Oath

"That's what love is. Love is keeping the promise anyway. Don't you believe in true love?"

John Green - The Fault in our Stars

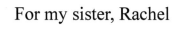

For my sister, Rachel

Eid des Hippokrates

*I swear by Apollo, the healer, Asclepius, Hygieia, and Panacea,
and I take to witness all the gods, all the goddesses, to keep
according to my ability and my judgment, the following Oath and
agreement:*
*To consider dear to me, as my parents, him who taught me this
art; to live in common with him and, if necessary, to share my
goods with him; To look upon his children as my own brothers,
to teach them this art; and that by my teaching, I will impart a
knowledge of this art to my own sons, and to my teacher's sons,
and to disciples bound by an indenture and oath according to the
medical laws, and no others.*
*I will prescribe regimens for the good of my patients according to
my ability and my judgment and never do harm to anyone.*
*I will give no deadly medicine to any one if asked, nor suggest
any such counsel; and similarly, I will not give a woman a pessa-
ry to cause an abortion.*
But I will preserve the purity of my life and my arts.
*I will not cut for stone, even for patients in whom the disease is
manifest; I will leave this operation to be performed by practi-
tioners, specialists in this art.*
*In every house where I come I will enter only for the good of my
patients, keeping myself far from all intentional ill-doing and all
seduction and especially from the pleasures of love with women
or men, be they free or slaves.*
*All that may come to my knowledge in the exercise of my pro-
fession or in daily commerce with men, which ought not to be
spread abroad, I will keep secret and will never reveal.*
*If I keep this oath faithfully, may I enjoy my life and practice my
art, respected by all humanity and in all times; but if I swerve
from it or violate it, may the reverse be my life.*

Chapter 1

Present day

Mum used to call me every night without fail. Sometimes it was a quick chat while I did the dishes, other times it turned into a long, rambling conversation that stretched late into the night. Occasionally, it was just a brief call to ask, "Hello, how is my Petal?" She always referred to me as "Petal" and never forgot about me.

I miss her dearly.

They say motherhood is the greatest gift from God, but for me, it was painful. I never got to experience it fully after Rebecca was taken away. The pain seeped into every aspect of my life, transforming me into a different person. I could never bring myself to tell Mum the truth, and that was the most distressing part. It forced me to lie and deceive her, which goes against my nature. No, that's not who I am, or at least so I used to believe.

And then, one day, she was gone. All I had left were memories and regrets. She left a void that remains unfilled, perhaps it will never be. Whenever the phone rings at night, my spirits rise momentarily, only to crash into my chest when I remember she's no longer here, burdening me with guilt.

One night, I was alone in the house, just before bedtime, when the phone rang. I was convinced it was her, even though I knew it was ridiculous. I answered and uttered, "Mum?"

I felt so foolish. I knew she was gone, gone forever. I remember slamming the phone down, angry at myself for being so silly, for desperately holding on to her memory. After she passed away, I felt immensely lonely, not just because she was gone, but also because of what happened all those years ago. I'm grateful she never witnessed the darker side of me and the events that unfolded.

But in truth, death and loss are natural occurrences. I've witnessed more than my fair share of death over the years. It's a natural part of being a doctor. Yet it never gets any easier, no matter what they say.

But enough of that. In a few moments, I'll be reunited with my own daughter.

Sitting at my desk, my hands are trembling uncontrollably. They are shaking so much I can hardly hold the interview papers.

I know that she won't recognise me, but I'll recognise her. I've seen her grow up, albeit mostly through photographs. Obviously, it's never the same, but that's all I had. It's all that was ever sent.

Okay... I believe I'm ready. Deep breath, Dr. Bowen-Wright. Here we go. Be brave.

"Mrs. Jenkins, could you please bring in Dr. Mueller?"

"I'm ready to interview her now."

1982

I never really had a strong desire to go to medical school. It wasn't my first choice; it just happened without much intention. I pursued it more to please Dad. When we're young, we often do things to please our parents rather than ourselves, or we focus solely on pleasing ourselves without considering our parents. It's usually one or the other.

At the age of eighteen, I had given up all hope of pursuing what I truly wanted: to be an artist. I had dreams of studying art at St Martin's College, immersing myself in the works of the great painters of the past, graduate, and wear my hair in red, henna-dyed locks, locks that were tousled and untidy, but in an alluring, captivating way. Well, that was my dream.

Then reality hit me—I would be poor. I would have nothing, absolutely nothing, and most importantly, I would have disappointed Mum and Dad. The demands of life jolted me awake. So, obediently, I enrolled in medical school armed with a bundle of A-levels and my brightest smile.

I vividly recall the interview. Mr. Mason, the admissions tutor, spent a significant amount of time asking me indirect questions and trying to peek down my blouse. I had an impressive cleavage back then. He wore a garish tweed jacket—the kind with synthetic leather patches on the elbows—paired with corduroy trousers and suede shoes.

"So, what will you bring to the medical profession?" I remember him saying, his tone polite yet condescending.

I remember looking away, absent-mindedly picking at my nails. I had a habit of picking at them then, usually trying to remove acrylic paint that stubbornly clung beneath my fingertips. I vaguely recall gazing up and replying, in a dreamy manner,

"Colour. I'll bring colour."

I have no idea if he grasped what I meant, but regardless, I received an offer, and Mr. Mason would spend another five years stealing glances at my chest while attempting to teach me endocrinology.

And so, Miss Kirstie McBride—I was McBride back then—left home and embarked on the journey of becoming a doctor. I was convinced it would fizzle out within a few weeks, and I would find myself back home with my paintings and my wonderfully eccentric mother. But somehow, it endured.

I can recall the day I left for university as vividly as if it were yesterday. I remember Mum and Dad waving goodbye at the National Express coach station in York. For some inexplicable reason, I chose the most convoluted bus route south simply because it was cheap. I had all my belongings, which weren't much, crammed into an old suitcase I'd bought in a charity shop. It was one of those vintage ones with a faux leather cover and plastic corner protectors. It reminded me of Paddington Bear's suitcase, only bigger and heavier.

God, it was an interminable journey—winding its way down the spine of Britain, stopping at every dreary town to pick up and drop passengers off, people who seemed even more destitute than me, and that's saying something. And yes, reflecting on my first days at university, they were an absolute disaster. A complete and utter train-wreck.

**

"Next stop, Eastleigh - Southampton," announced the bus driver.

I glanced at him with a questioning look, but he paid no attention.

"Eastleigh - Southampton," he repeated sternly.

"Thanks," I replied uncertainly, offering him a smile.

His fingers drummed incessantly on the steering wheel, indicating his impatience. He opened the doors and nodded towards the exit, as if making a solemn judgment. I smiled back, but again it had no effect.

Something didn't feel right. I had travelled down on the train before, but this seemed different. Reluctantly, I tossed my suitcase onto the pavement.

I immediately regretted it.

The case hit the ground, bursting open like an overripe orange splattering across a kitchen floor. In a burst of colour, my clothes and underwear scattered all over the forecourt like a rainbow coloured firework going off.

Embarrassed, I jumped off the bus, landing awkwardly on my bad ankle.

"Christ-All-Mighty!" I cried out, looking up for a bit of sympathy.

But unsurprisingly the bus had gone. I was alone.

All I could hear was the rumble of its engine as it faded into the distance. I noticed a few small children waving mockingly at me from the rear window. Perhaps I gave them a V sign back, but I can't recall; it was so long ago. If I did, they probably deserved it.

The noise of the bus finally dissipated into silence.

I felt and looked like a complete mess, the aftermath of a long-distance coach journey. I felt like shit. My hair was dishevelled and my face flushed and creased from resting against the window the last ten miles. Catching my refection in the bus-stop hoarding it looked as if I had just been slapped.

There I was, hobbling around like a madwoman, desperately trying to retrieve my belongings from the ground before they flew off into the distance. It was the last thing I needed as I took my first fledgling steps toward becoming a doctor.

Well, no. Let me take a step back for a moment.

The last thing I needed was some stranger offering to help pick up my underwear.

I had no idea where he came from; he simply appeared out of nowhere.

"Quickly, before they all blow away and you'll have none!" he shouted.

I was so taken aback, I didn't dare look up.

"It's okay, I've got them," I replied.

"Honestly, do you want a hand?"

I didn't respond.

I suddenly felt petrified, clutching a handful of my underwear in my trembling hand.

Summoning some courage, I glanced up.

I expected to see a much older man. He would later confess that his heavy smoking of 'The Bensons' made him as he would say, sound more mature. He was in his twenties, just like me. It made it even more embarrassing.

As I crouched on the floor, I gazed up like a curious puppy.

"Umm... skinny legs," I thought, maybe I said it out loud. Frankly, I was exhausted, and to be honest, I can't remember.

He made a grunt, but I would later learn that he tended to grunt when his mind was overwhelmed, which was often. However, he did have nice legs and a kind face. I mustered some strength and continued stuffing my crumpled laundry back into the case, even though now it seemed impossible to fit it all back in.

Suddenly a pair of my better knickers caught a gust of wind and transformed into a little pink-brown kite, soaring across the forecourt.

He nodded in the general direction, as if to say, "Go after them, girl!"

"I'm not chasing after my own knickers! I'm not that desperate!" I exploded.

He smiled, evidently thinking something impolite but wisely choosing not to say it.

Finally, I managed to close the suitcase and stood up, attempting to gather myself.

As darkness fell, the sun was setting and the chill creeping in. I gave the young man an insincere smile.

He was rake thin, with one of those acid-washed denim jackets that were all the rage in the eighties. Combined with a faded *Talking Heads* t-shirt that seemed to have endured a thousand washes, and a hint of a mullet hairstyle he was quite a sight.

Reflecting on it now, it was quite comical. Though, to be frank, my own attire was probably no better. I believe I was wearing a pair of torn leggings, khaki shorts, and my beloved burgundy cardigan, which I permanently wore those days. I adored that cardigan.

"Do you know where Highfield Road is?" I asked, trying to find my bearings. "It's in Southampton."

"No, this is Eastleigh," he replied.

"Eastleigh?"

"Yes, Eastleigh, near Southampton," he clarified, struggling to light his cigarette.

"How near?"

"Near as in a short car journey," he responded.

"Fucking hell!"

"Language," he chided, still fumbling with his cigarette.

I let out a sigh and kicked my case. Its contents burst open again and another piece of my laundry escaped into the wild.

"Fuck-in-hell!"

"I was sure I said Southampton." I muttered, engaging in a little argument with myself.

"You can take a train," he interjected.

I glared at him, feeling an overwhelming urge to tell him to fuck off, but I restrained myself. After all, he was only trying to help. He gazed back at me, his expression revealing a lack of concern either way.

"I don't have enough money for a train," I finally admitted, feeling a sense of embarrassment, avoiding eye contact.

"I suppose you're a bit short on undies as well?" he teased.

And for the first of many times, Dave Hudson, part-time barman, mechanic, and juggler of various other odd jobs, made me laugh.

"I can give you a lift to Highfield if you want. It's on my way. I live in Shirley," he offered.

"Where's that?" I asked, eyeing him up and down.

"Just outside Southampton."

I scrutinised him for a moment. I had been away from home for less than eight hours and here I was considering accepting a ride from some strange, scruffy bloke I had just met.

"Why are you at a coach station if you have a car?" I asked.

"Cos I've just seen my girlfriend off,"

"What's her name?" I continued probing.

"Debbie,"

"Prove it." I challenged.

He looked at me, exasperated.

"I don't have to prove to a woman I've just met that I have a bloody girlfriend!"

He had a point, although being called a woman when I was only eighteen felt a bit strange.

"So, why are you here?" he asked turning the tables.

"I'm starting at the university next week," I replied, feeling a twinge of self-consciousness.

"At the medical school in Southampton."

"Yeah, thought you were a student," he replied, taking a big, drag from his cigarette.

He offered it to me. I declined.

"Of course, cancer sticks and all that," he said, shuffling on his feet.

He stood there, puffing on his cigarette, blowing a cloud of grey smoke into the air.

I didn't know what to do.

The silence stretched out uncomfortably, making me consider picking up my luggage and finding a phone to call someone, although I wasn't quite sure who.

Finally, with no other choice, I gave in.

"Thanks, I'd love a lift," I said, mustering another forced smile.

"Top one!" he replied enthusiastically. He then tossed his cigarette to the ground, extinguishing it with a twist of his shoe, and swiftly grabbed my suitcase with his other hand.

Then he was off, moving faster than I had anticipated. I had to practically run to keep up. My initial worry was that he might steal my case, but the idea was absurd considering the worthless junk I had hauled from home. If he's a thief, he's not a very good one, or a very unlucky one, I reasoned, calming myself down.

So, after a day-long coach journey, I found myself chasing after a weird man, that resembled a Glastonbury roadie, across a darkening car-park to God knows where.

A great start, Kirstie, a great start.

I stumbled behind him, attempting to fix my hair with one hand while tugging my cardigan down to cover myself with the other.

Then he turned a corner, and finally, we arrived.

"Voila!" he exclaimed, adding a flourish of his hand to emphasize his exclamation.

"Oh!" I replied.

His car was an absolute wreck.

I recall it being red, a Vauxhall Nova if I'm not mistaken, or at least it used to be red. The paintwork on the bonnet had been stripped back and covered up with what appeared to be a botched attempt at a re-spray, likely done by a blind man. The bonnet now sported a washed-out, almost matte pink hue. Countless dents marred the bodywork. I'd seen dodgem cars in better shape.

Most of the holes had been filled with putty, poorly sanded, and spray-painted with primer, leaving the job half done. When I got to know him better I realised that was one of his monikers: "Job-Left-Half-Done Dave"

I stood gawping at the vehicle. He dropped my case to the ground.

From the look of disappointment on my face, he could tell there was a stark contrast between my expectations and the reality before me.

"It looks better in the daylight," he reassured me.

I nodded sagely, pretending to possess knowledge about cars, which I certainly didn't.

"It just needs a bit of work on the outside, but the engine's in good shape. I know my motors me," he boasted.

I stepped towards the rear of the vehicle, waiting for him to skip around and pop the boot open. He didn't.

"No, the boot's fucked, won't open. You'll have to toss your stuff on the back seat,"

"Thanks... Sorry... Um... I didn't get your name?" I said in that typical embarrassed English manner we have when we want to ask something but fear it might be too intrusive.

He responded matter-of-factly, which was refreshing. His straightforward, no-nonsense approach would grow on me.

"Dave. Most people call me Dave," he replied, as if it hardly mattered to him.

"Alright, I'll go along with the majority and call you Dave as well."

"And yours?" he inquired.

Here's what struck me as weird: I distinctly remember telling him my name and it felt somewhat strange. Now he knew something about me, well, at least my first name, but it somehow changed everything. Perhaps it was because my anonymity had suddenly vanished.

"Kirstie. My name's Kirstie," I said.

He hummed, as if pondering something.

I climbed into the car, and he started the engine. From the mechanical coughing, it was clear it wasn't in the best shape. Dave sucked air through his teeth and muttered something under his breath. Then suddenly we lurched forward.

Then it was silent, except for the engine, which sounded like it was running without any oil in the system.

"Does that noise sound alright to you?" I asked.

"Completely normal," he replied. "Completely normal."

It didn't sound it.

Then it hit me. He could have been taking me anywhere. He might have been leading me to some dark woods to rape and dismember me, for all I knew. I started picking at my nails and staring out of the grimy windows, which were in desperate need of cleaning, working myself into a state of anxiety once again.

I thought of my Mum, who was probably doing the dishes about now, while chattering away to Dad, who, truth be told, probably wouldn't be paying the slightest bit of attention but interjecting with "quite right, dear" at all the appropriate moments to maintain the illusion that he was listening. I was missing them already.

Just as my worries began to escalate, he asked the oddest of questions.

"Do you like cats?"

"What?" I replied.

"Do you like cats?" he repeated.

"I haven't really thought about it much. I had a rabbit once, and I used to ride..."

"Ride?" he interrupted, confused.

"Yes, ride a horse," I clarified.

"Oh."

"But you don't have anything against cats, right?"

"No, why do you ask?"

"No reason, just curious," he responded, now lost in thought.

I looked at him, puzzled. He didn't take any notice and simply stared ahead at the road.

More silence followed. But at least we were talking, so I decided to keep the conversation going.

"Do you like cats?" I asked him.

He turned to me as if I had crossed a line in the sand.

"No, I bloody hate the little bastards!"

"Little inquisitive bastards - licking their own arses," he added.

"I'm more of a dog person myself," I chimed in, pretending that it didn't really matter.

"I've always wanted a dog," he whispered to himself.

After that, we fell back into silence. Maybe I had upset him. I stared out of the window.

Thirty minutes later, we arrived at my lodgings, which appeared as inviting as the amount of money I could afford for my first night's stay, which wasn't much.

He looked up at the sign above the entrance.

"Heaton Place - B&B," the sign said, or it would have if half the letters hadn't been missing.

"Highfield is quite posh," he commented. "...but this place looks a bit..."

"...of a complete shit-hole?" I added, finishing his sentence.

"A bit tired," he said diplomatically.

"Well, it's all I can afford," I replied, then remembered it was none of his business.

Sensing the awkwardness of the moment, he leapt out of the car.

I thought he was about to help me retrieve my suitcase from the back seat, but being the gentleman he was, he didn't. Then, seeing that I was struggling to pull it out myself, he intervened, manhandled the case, and dropped it on the ground. It nearly popped open again.

I glared at him, but he paid no attention.

"Well, good luck with the medicine,"

"Medical school. I'm studying medicine, not taking it," I corrected him.

"Yeah, right - keep saying it," he replied, turning to get back into the car.

Then he stopped. He swivelled around as if anchored to the pavement.

"If you're looking for a place to stay, I've got a mate who's got a spare room with a reasonable rent. It's in a shared house, not far from the Uni. I've heard it's bloody immaculate. Right up your street,"

I glared at him, incredulous.

"Anyway, have a look if you want. It's up to you, Love,"

My glare became a scowl. Love - indeed.

He scribbled an address on a dirty piece of paper, which he pulled from his back pocket, and handed it to me.

"Thanks," I replied unconvincingly.

I stuffed the grubby note into my cardie pocket. Cheeky bugger! I mustered an attempt at a smile.

Dave grinned back, got into the car, and slammed the door. All the windows rattled. He lowered his window and stuck his head out.

"You take care now. Get yourself to that knicker-shop bloody pronto," he said with a wink, and sped off, leaving me outside the B&B.

Then suddenly, I was alone again.

I looked up at the house. The window curtains were drawn. Gray, lace-net curtains adorned the upper floor windows, reminiscent of the ones my Nana used to have in her house, nets that had fallen out of fashion in the '60s. Frankly, they appeared as if they had been hanging in the windows since then. They looked absolutely filthy.

The whole place was as welcoming as the sign. But I had no choice, and besides I would only be staying there for a week - or so I thought - and frankly, I was dead on my feet.

I knocked on the door.

"Breakfast is served at eight o'clock, at the very latest. Don't expect anything after that, as it'll all be put away. No guests in your room, please. This is a B&B, not a knocking shop. If you are out after eleven, you'll have to use the rear door. And no music after nine pm. My husband and I retire very, very early,"

I was wrong. The place was even less welcoming than the sign. The landlady proceeded to recite an additional set of rules for nearly five minutes without taking a breath. She delivered the words mechanically, much like a disinterested waitresses reciting the menu to customers they didn't really give a sod about.

I was too tired to care. I let the stipulations wash over me.

"This is your room. Please don't play with the radiator controls, as George has only just bled the system," she continued.

"Thanks," I replied, "you've been very kind. This room will be fine."

Mrs. Marshall glared at me, seemingly surprised by my gratitude, suspecting that I was mocking her. Giving me the benefit of the doubt, she handed me the key.

"Remember, breakfast finishes at eight," she reiterated, and abruptly left the room, slamming the door behind her.

I stood and surveyed the room. It seemed frozen in the 1970s. The carpet was a mishmash of colours, thankfully faded since it had been laid. The walls were adorned with wallpaper featuring delicate oriental etchings against an embossed background. Nailed to the wall opposite a tiny bed were three porcelain swallows, arranged in a wonky formation against an oriental sky. Each bird was slightly askew, giving the impression that they were all flying whilst a bit drunk.

I plopped myself onto the edge of the narrowest single bed I had ever seen.

Then, uncontrollably, tears began streaming down my face. Loneliness engulfed me. It suddenly struck me I was on my own; for the first time in my life.

All I could think of was my parents waving me off at the coach station. Mum pretending not to cry by incessantly blowing her nose, as Dad scratched the back of his head, a nervous habit of his that served the same purpose. I remember them continuing to wave until the bus turned the corner.

I so longed to anywhere else than there.

So, as I always did when I felt down: I sketched.

Retrieving my charcoal and pencils from the bottom of my suitcase, I propped myself up on the bed, with my knees practically tucked under my chin, and began drawing. Without any reason, I sketched the landlady, envisioning her as a pointy-hatted witch straight out of the Wizard of Oz. After fifteen minutes, I completed the sketch, feeling a bit of release.

I tossed the sketchbook onto the bedside table, slipped under the sheets still fully clothed, and attempted to sleep. Tomorrow would be another day, I reassured myself. I set my alarm but then changed my mind and turned it off. I would sleep in tomorrow. Sod her bloody breakfast.

**

The accommodation noticeboard was barren of adverts. Hoping for at least some options, I approached the Student Union office. The student representative, more focused on her crossword puzzle in the newspaper than helping me, didn't bother looking up when I asked.

"The accommodation board? Have you moved it? The one near reception doesn't have much on it,"

"Too late. All the good rooms are gone," she replied dismissively, without even lifting her gaze.

"Damn it!"

My outburst finally caught her attention, prompting her to set down her copy of the Daily Mirror and acknowledge me.

"Sorry, term starts next week. If you haven't found anything by now, you're out of luck."

"Nothing at all? Seriously?"

"You could wait until The Echo comes out next Thursday. Maybe there will be some new listings then."

I let out a deflated sigh.

"I'm sorry. There might still be some crappy options left on the board, but honestly, if they're still available, you'd be better off pitching a tent on The Common until something decent comes up."

My heart sank.

She sensed my despair.

"Something will come up," she offered, attempting to feign concern.

I stared at her in disbelief.

"Look, after the second week, there are usually drop-outs, homesickness and all that. Come back in two weeks."

I thanked her, although she didn't seem to notice, as her focus returned to her beloved crossword puzzle.

I didn't have two weeks. Feeling despondent, I trudged back to the B&B to figure out my next move. However, upon arriving, the decision had already been made for me.

**

What struck me when I saw Rebecca up close was how remarkably clean and fresh her complexion was. Honestly, I couldn't even tell if she was wearing makeup, and also by the resemblance between us, particularly with our slightly flushed cheekbones, with a faint hint of the oriental. I wasn't sure where they came from, some genetic throwback that fades with time, I've been told.

There was something in our similarity that seemed to unsettle her. I could sense it in her eyes. Nevertheless, she carried on with a calm composure that I expected from her.

She had her ginger hair pulled back into a tight and neat ponytail that cascaded over her shoulder. I caught myself wondering if she dyed it. Which was a bit mean-spirited, given my own henna dyed locks as a student.

When we shook hands, I felt the absence of her fingertip. I tried my best not to stare at it. Maybe she became aware of my glances because she folded her middle finger beneath her palm, cradling her hands with perfect composure on her lap as she spoke.

The interview unfolded in the usual meandering manner of all my interviews, where I explored where each answer would go and tried to understand the driving force behind the candidate. I needed to understand Rebecca's beliefs, her principles, and the boundaries she wouldn't cross. These were usually the things that mattered to me.

But this time it was different.

In truth, I didn't really care. Rebecca was going to get the job no matter what.

"As I mentioned, my passion lies in Primary Care," she answered my question with complete confidence.

It was the first time I had heard her speak, aside from a brief phone conversation. Her accent was elusive, an English accent with a slight over-articulation that hinted at her education in various private schools across Europe. Yes, she had been well-educated.

While she spoke, I wasn't listening to her words. I was simply captivated, overwhelmed by the proximity to her after all this time. My eyes absorbed every detail of her features. The urge to reach out and touch her was almost irresistible.

**

When I returned to the B&B, I thought things couldn't possibly get any worse.

But, unfortunately, they did. Mrs. Marshall was waiting for me, ready to pounce as soon as I entered. I assumed it was because I had missed her precious breakfast. She stood there, glaring at me with a disgusted expression on her face, as if she had just tasted something foul.

"What is this?" she shrieked, shoving the sketch under my nose.

I looked at it and back up at her, impressing myself how accurate the likeness was.

"I'm sorry. It's just a silly drawing. I didn't mean to offend you," I replied, even though it was a lie.

In truth, I did intend to offend her.

She pursed her lips, as if summoning some sort of spell, and then took a deep breath, seemingly preparing to make a pronouncement.

"Well, my dear, this will be your last night here. I simply cannot tolerate vagabonds like you in my establishment. I am not here to be insulted !"

Being called a vagabond for the first time was unexpected, but I had a feeling it wouldn't be the last.

I could feel my anger welling up inside me. I took a moment to consider my options. Should I apologise a bit more? Express greater remorse?

No.

I was young and had a rather short temper back then to put it mildly. I decided to give her a piece of my mind, just as Mum would have done.

"That's fine with me."

"Frankly, I'm not impressed with your little shit-pit of a B&B anyway,"

She looked at me as though I had just punched her.

Without another word I stormed up to my room, grabbed my suitcase, lugged it down the stairs and marched out the front door.

She stood there as if a bucket of cold water had been thrown over her.

"..and fixing your fucking sign outside would be a good place to start!" I shouted back, before turning and heading off, leaving her slack-jawed in the doorway.

I didn't even look back.

When you find yourself in a hole, Kirstie, just keep digging, I thought to myself.

As for where I was heading. Well, I wasn't quite sure

Chapter 2

With an air of inevitability, I found myself standing outside 34a Percy Road, Shirley.

I gazed up at the pebble-dashed exterior. It was almost lunchtime, and all the curtains remained tightly closed. I would later discover that the curtains at 34a Percy Road were never opened, I mean never. It wasn't because there were any secret activities or hidden cannabis farms within its drab and unremarkable facade. No, it was simply because the occupants of this house, being blokes, couldn't be bothered to open them.

I pressed the doorbell, but nothing happened. Trying harder, I pressed it again with my thumb. Still, no response. I sighed, which was now becoming a bit of a habit.

I stood there, contemplating my predicament—no place to stay , no grant check yet, and a dwindling supply of clean underwear—it seemed things couldn't possibly get any worse. Maybe I should have stayed home.

Then, from an upstairs window, a head appeared.

"Top one," he whispered down.

"Look, I've come about the room!" I shouted up.

"Shush... I'll let you in,"

After a few seconds of crashing sounds from within, he finally opened the porch door. I think he fell down the stairs, but he denied it later. Dave stood before me, wearing the same t-shirt he had worn yesterday and a pair of underpants. Sensing my unease, he looked down at his bare legs.

"Sorry, Got a big wash on."

"So, you're the one who lives here, not your mate?" I asked, trying to steer the conversation forward and way from his semi-naked state.

"Sort of," he said replied sheepishly. Then suddenly he grabbed my arm, pulling me across the porch — which desperately needed tidying — and dragged me into the hall.

He put his finger to his lips. "Shush... Gavin's on nights. He's sleeping."

He made a childish gesture, pressing his palms against his cheek to signify sleep. Later, I would learn that when Dave got stressed as well as grunting, he preferred using gestures instead of words as his brain couldn't cope.

"Don't want to wake Gav. He's on nights at the docks. He gets pretty angry if I wake him up."

I nodded, pretending to fully grasp the situation. Subsequently, I discovered that Gavin could get away with almost anything because he was "on nights".

Dave led me into the living room, and that's when I noticed the cats.

Cats were everywhere—one on the table, one on the sofa, even one sleeping on top of the television.

"I thought you hated cats?"

"I do," he replied.

"They're dirty creatures," he continued. "Do you know how much time they spend licking their arses?"

"Yes, you told me," I replied.

"I would never want to lick my arse, even if I could," he said, shaking his head.

I was more surprised by the fact that he had contemplated the theoretical possibility of licking his own backside, than by his same conclusion about the cats. Later, I would realise that Dave spent a lot of time pondering imaginary scenarios—situations that could never happen—instead of dealing with the practical aspects of daily life, such as washing, dressing, and cleaning.

"Even if I could reach my own backside, I still wouldn't," he emphasized, gesturing with his hands to convey his strong aversion to the idea.

"I've come about the room," I interjected, attempting to redirect the conversation to the present moment.

"Oh, yes, the room," he replied, back on track.

He grabbed my wrist a little too tightly, and pulled me up the stairs. The steps were cluttered and covered in general mess; characteristic of a house inhabited by slobs. With the excitement of a young child, he almost dragged me to the landing.

Releasing my wrist, he nudged the door open with his knee, signalling for me to be quiet with his finger.

I braced myself for the worst: a dilapidated room with a dirty carpet, a sweaty bed, and the unmistakable smell of a house occupied by unwashed men.

But it was nothing like that at all.

The room was immaculate, clean enough to impress my mum. The bed looked brand new, and the cream-coloured walls were bare. The wardrobe seemed decent too.

"No cats allowed in here," Dave declared.

I stared at him, slightly confused. "So, what's the deal with the cats?" I inquired.

"The landlady's mother, who used to live here, passed away a few years ago. One stipulation in her will was that the cats stayed with the house,"

"Can't stand the creatures," he reiterated, as if it had been at all unclear to me.

"This room looks pretty decent. The rest of the house... well, it's a bit chaotic," I remarked tactfully.

Dave was silent for a second, and looked as if he want to say something, but unsure how. Then with a sigh.

"This is where she popped her clogs. Messy business apparently, very upsetting. Dead for a month and nobody noticed. The landlady stripped the room bare after she pegged it, to sort of move on, I think."

"Oh." I replied not knowing what to say for a moment.

That sort of took the edge off the splendour of the room, a room that looked an oasis of order and cleanliness in a desert of clutter, now tainted by death.

Even Dave sensed I wasn't too comfortable.

"Maybe I shouldn't have told you?"

I looked at him. He looked like a schoolboy who had just blabbed to the teacher.

21

I sighed.

"Well, let's pretend you never did."

I went through my options and there were only two: accept this room or go back home to my parents. I really needed a place to stay. I could always move on if it got a bit creepy I thought to myself, trying to justify it all.

"I'll take it." I said with a smile.

Dave bounced around on his tiptoes with excitement.

"Top one!" he burst out, punching air with his fist, as if he had just won on a fruit machine.

"Shall I show you the rest of the house?'" he spluttered, skipping down the stairs.

I obediently followed, still a bit unsure about the whole thing.

He led me into the kitchen.

"This area could do with a wee bit of a tidy" he commented in a matter-of-fact manner, as if he was an estate agent.

On entering, I could see the embarrassment on his face.

"A wee bit of a tidy!" I said nearly choking.

The kitchen was an absolute bloody mess. It was hygienically dangerous. It was an absolute shit-pit. Plates upon plates of unwashed dishes were stacked on top of each other, everywhere. The waste bin was overflowing. I could smell it from the door.

Not one square-inch of the work-surface wasn't covered with something that had just been left, should have been thrown away, or had been there so long it was now part of the kitchen. A cat was licking the remains of food left on a discarded plate. She looked clearly put out at being disturbed and gave me a glare of disapproval.

"Has this kitchen ever been cleaned?"

He glanced around at the mess as if seeing it for the first time, clearly ashamed.

"Of course!"

I glowered at him.

"Yes, absolutely. You've just come at the wrong time, caught us on a bad day. It's usually spick-and-span."

I gave him another scowl.

"Well, sorry to inconvenience you, but I'm not staying in a house that's a health hazard. Cats I can live with, but dirty, lazy blokes, I can't. If I'm staying here, I want this cleaned. Pronto."

I was using my best headmistress voice and Dave knew it.

"Here's your key then.' he said changing the subject. 'Rent is fifty pounds a week, all in."

I took the key and continued my lecture.

"I'll be back in a few hours. When I get back, I want this kitchen clean."

I stopped just short from adding, - Do I make myself clear? -, as I thought it would have been a bit much on the first day.

"Of course." Dave replied, unconvincingly.

Then I left Dave to stew for a bit and hopefully start defusing his hygiene time-bomb before it exploded.

**

When I returned three hours later, I had hoped he'd have made at least a symbolic effort. A few plates having been washed would have satisfied me. Just a few, not many. I would have even accepted him throwing just some of the shit out. Just to show he knew I was in the right, and he was a dirty, messy slob.

But, no.

If anything the kitchen was in a worse state than when I had left it.

In my absence, 'Gav on Nights' had left his breakfast dishes on top of the tottering tower of waste, and then gone off to be 'on nights'.

Where they'd got all the dishes from was a mystery to me.

My blood was absolutely boiling.

"Why is this mess still here?" I shouted up the stairs.

But all I could hear was, 'Spandau Ballet, Instinction' blaring out from one of the bedrooms.

I stood there aghast at the mess.

Well, the more fool me; it started with one plate. I had to clear the sink to wash that one and make a little clean area for it to drain. Once I cleaned one, there was no going back. The one clean plate shone like a beacon of spotlessness in the kitchen, and I had a compulsion to do another.

One became two, then a dozen, and soon I had a stack of dripping wet, soapy clean plates draining on the worktop. I stood back and admired them. Sadly, they only made the surrounding filth look worse, insulting my efforts. The only way forward was for my little clean territory, to get bigger. I pressed on.

Once I started, I got a bit of a rhythm going. Anything that looked beyond hope went straight into a rubbish bag, which was about half of the contents of the kitchen. Suddenly after two hours, which flashed by, low and behold, was a clean, tidy, and rather presentable kitchen.

Just as I finished, Dave stumbled in, singing *Spandau* to himself.

"Wow!"

I smiled at him, as I was quite pleased with it myself.

"'Wow!" he repeated, "Top one!"

"You beat me to it. I was just coming down to, well, get stuck in."

I shot him another of my schoolmistress stares.

"Dave don't push your luck. One dirty plate out of place and I'm off."

It was early days in my fractious relationship with Dave, so I was a bit restrained, but I think he got the message. I could tell by him gulping, and not saying anything.

"No worries."

Then he was gone, bouncing back up the stairs.

I stood in the kitchen and smiled to myself.

On reflection, I should have milked those happy, carefree moments as much as I could, before they were gone. But back then I didn't know the cruel cards fate would deal me. I just lived each untroubled day, one day at a time.

**

"This is your office,"
"Thank you. You've been very kind. Too kind,"
"Too kind? Certainly not. I understand what it's like to start in General Practice. It's a significant change."

She looked around the room and smiled, a self-congratulatory smile, I thought.

Deciding to test the waters, I asked, "Will you be moving down to Poole with your partner?"

I noticed a flash behind her eyes, a strange mix of hurt and embarrassment, and something else I couldn't quite place.

"No. No, I'm single," she abruptly replied, composing herself.

As I looked into her eyes, I saw the same eyes as mine and the same upright posture as her father's. Was she lying? I would have been able to tell if my own daughter wasn't telling the truth, surely? All good mothers can.

But there's a catch—I wasn't one. Well, not in my eyes.

'Yes, that's quite right. Let's focus on the future. My apologies for assuming and prying," I replied.

I was hoping she would reassure me with a response like, 'No, it's not a problem.'

But she didn't.

She smiled insincerely and gazed around the Treatment Room. I watched her with pent-up emotion, observing her every gesture, searching for any clue she knew more than she was letting on, but she revealed nothing.

She appeared pleased as she surveyed the room.

Curiosity got the better of me, and I asked, "I noticed from your application that you did your training abroad?"

Suddenly, she came alive, and her cheeks flushed, not from a nerve I had touched, but from excitement. In an instant she almost

25

became another person.

"Yes, Heidelberg," she gushed.

"It was lovely. Heidelberg is such a beautiful city. I trained at the University; it was...'

Her voice trailed off into silence, as if she had remembered something.

"Yes, it was magical," she finally continued. "I spent five years training and studying at the University."

"That must have been wonderful?"

"Yes, I went there to study. My parents used to take me there on holiday when I was young. I fell in love with the city. My mother still lives there now."

I flinched, but I don't think she even noticed.

"Can I call you Kirstie?" she asked changing tack.

"Of course, you can. We're very informal here."

"And you, where did you do your training?"

"I studied in Southampton. Feels like ages ago now," I replied, noticing her self-consciously biting her lip as I spoke.

Then there was an uncomfortable pause.

"I'll let you settle in," I said, eager to return to my office.

"Let me know if you need anything."

"Thank you. You've been very kind," she repeated, offering a weak smile.

Back in my office, I couldn't take it anymore. I closed the door and turned on the red consultation light. The pressure of emotions built up like water behind a dam, pressing, pressing. Memories returned like images escaping from a sealed box—memories locked away for many years.

I sat there, listening to the sound of my panting breath, the ticking clock, and the pounding headache from the excesses of the night before. Why couldn't I bloody stop?

I reminded myself that this was the first step to getting her back, getting her back for good. I had to work this through. Be strong Kirstie. Was I doing the right thing? I didn't know. But I had no one else I could trust, except for Gus.

**

One of the memories I have from my early days at medical school is the drinking. It always struck me as ironic that medical students, who are supposed to eventually preach against excessive alcohol consumption, were often the ones indulging the most. Perhaps the rationale is to get the drinking out of the way before having to lecture others on the harms of booze.

I certainly can attest to the deep-rooted culture of drinking within the medical profession. When Rebecca was taken away, I turned to drink as a coping mechanism. Alcohol become my crutch, a sedative to make it all go away rather than face up to things.

At the time she was taken, I was still training to become a Registrar. Looking back now, I realise that I fitted the description of a "functioning alcoholic,". On the surface, I appeared calm and composed, but beneath it all, I was plagued by self-doubt, low self-esteem, and a turbulent personal life. I would drink excessively every night to escape it all, and surprisingly, I was still able to perform adequately as a doctor during the day—at least that's how it appeared, or so I thought.

Then the instructions arrived, and everything changed, well, almost. I had to focus on following them, or else. Alcohol could only numb so much, and when the demands came, I directed my attention towards these. It was my only way out, and in a perverted sense, those tasks probably saved my life, giving me a purpose.

But in the early days, it was a different story altogether. Drinking was a source of pleasure for me, as it was for everyone else. I relished every hazy, confused, and fuzzy moment of it. It was during one of these wild drinking sessions that I fell for Marky. Though, initially, I found him utterly infuriating.

I would like to say that I remember that night vividly, but that would be a lie. I was completely smashed, almost to the point of blackout. It all started in the Student Bar during "Happy Hour," - although that term was misleading in two ways. Firstly, the half-priced drinks lasted for ninety minutes, and secondly, the happiness associated with them was just superficial.

I'm not exactly sure how the conversation began, but it revolved around the "environment" and how we were damaging the planet. This was during a time when the concept of global warming was still new and considered outrageous. At the time, I was an angry environmentalist, wholeheartedly buying into the whole narrative. And to my irritation, Marky casually mentioned that he drove his car every day, covering a mere three-mile distance from his place to the University. It triggered my anger, amplified by the four pints of strong cider I had consumed in less than an hour.

Marky was older than me and pursuing a PhD in a subject I didn't comprehend then, and honestly, I still don't. Not because I'm unintelligent, but because I was different from Marky. I was connected to the real world, where I witnessed people in pain and suffering, while his work seemed theoretical, hypothetical, and filled with mathematical nonsense. Of course, I never expressed this opinion to his face. Marky possessed qualities that I lacked— he was tall, quiet, with untamed black hair that never seemed to require trimming. He was thoughtful, his views were considered, and he spoke softly. In short, he embodied everything that I was not.

Every week, we exchanged lingering glances in the bar, engaging in silent conversations that nobody else could perceive. As the night progressed, my frustration grew, and our flirting became more intense, if you catch my drift.

His shyness was endearing, and it made me adore him even more. At times, his vulnerability touched my heart, but on other occasions, it drove me up the wall. I would urge him to "man up," yet he would surprise me by assuming complete control with an unexpected display of self-confidence. He was a paradox, and I would love him for it.

Writing this all now, I realise how much I still miss him, but also blame completely for what happened.

That night, he taunted me, claiming that he could get home faster than I could with his car. I was incensed.

I had just acquired a brand new yellow mountain bike, one of the trends at the time, which I cherished dearly. Deep down, I knew it was stolen, although I kept telling myself otherwise. I was in denial about so many things back then, until that moment.

**

"What? You think you'll get back to Shirley faster than me? Are you joking?" I retorted.

"Kirstie, I have a car, and you only have a bicycle," he replied.

That dismissive comment about "just having a bicycle" ignited my anger further. I stared into his chestnut brown eyes, torn between the conflicting desires to either punch him in the face or kiss him. And given my drunken state, anger won.

"Fuck you! I'll see you in Shirley. The last one back pays for drinks all next week!" I replied, slamming my pint glass onto the table a little too forcefully, the remaining cider splashing out.

Everyone around us turned to look, and there was that brief moment of awkwardness that drunk people don't notice, but everyone else does—the kind of moment that becomes a topic of conversation the next day.

Unsteadily, I stood up and announced, "I'm leaving. Thank you, everybody."

Later, a close friend discreetly told me that no one paid much attention to my departure, and it was a bit, well, embarrassing.

I stumbled into the cool autumn night. The lights seemed brighter and sharper due to my intoxication. Him and his damn car! I was determined to prove a point. I was going to beat him. I was certain of it. So, I left the School of Biological Sciences, unlocked my bike, and clumsily mounted it.

In my mind, I was determined to win, although in reality, I was far from capable. Marky approached and stood nearby, completely sober. He was about to witness the action of a madwoman. Standing unsteadily on my feet, I perched on the saddle with my hands on the handlebars, the bike serving as a stabilizer I swayed side to side. I was ready to race a man I didn't yet know I loved, all while being completely and utterly smashed.

And ever the gentleman, Marky let me. He even gave me a head start.

So, off I raced. I remember him shouting 'stupid bitch' at me as I left.

Looking back at it now, it all seemed so silly and pointless. But as I said, I had a bit of a temper back then.

I was off.

The cold night air rushed against my burning cheeks as I sped away. I felt invincible. I pushed the pedals with all my might, as I zipped down Winchester Road towards Shirley. There was no way he could catch me. I was going to teach that smug petrol-head a lesson.

Then the harsh reality of fitness hit me—the moment when you're drunk and suddenly realise it. Driven solely by the power of cider and lacking any real leg-strength or endurance, the absurdity of the challenge became apparent. With each passing yard, my speed suddenly decreased as my lungs threatened to burst. Beads of sweat and alcohol oozed from my forehead into the night air.

Inevitably, I heard him approaching, honking like a madman.

"Fuck you!" I screamed. "You complete and utter jerk!"

I raised my middle finger in defiance.

Then I realised it wasn't Marky, but rather someone in a Rover, admonishing my lack of lights, road sense, and general instability. I shouted—or slurred—an apology as they passed, giving me a wide berth.

Then, the adrenaline kicked back in.

Invigorated, I pedalled on. But, within moments, he had caught up. Through his car's windscreen, I could see his smug grin, a look of satisfaction and self-importance.

He sped past me.

Fuelled by alcohol, foolishness, and youthful idiocy, I had a secret weapon: traffic lights.

Traffic lights would be my friend. I giggled at the sheer absurdity of the idea. Dangerously, but too intoxicated to care, I breezed through every set of red lights from the University to my lodgings. I could feel his frustration growing as he waited for the lights to change as I zipped past him. Minute by minute, fuelled by my own recklessness, I distanced myself from him. After what seemed an age of frenzied pedalling, I was nearly there. I rounded the bend to my house, punched the air in celebration and nearly came off my bike.

Suddenly he was back.

Then he did something that instantly sobered me up.

He tried to force me off the road with his car!

I swerved onto the pavement to protect myself, coming to an unsteady stop outside my house. His car screeched to a halt, half on the pavement and half on the road.

All I could hear was my panting breath as I tried to recover.

"Are you trying to fucking kill me, or what? You complete and utter twat!" I screamed in gasps.

He stumbled out of the car, his face flushed with anger, looking like a man possessed. He slammed the car door shut as hard as he could.

"I thought you wanted to kill yourself? You stupid bitch! I was just trying to scare you,"

"Well, it damn well worked, you wanker!" I bellowed, my voice suddenly hoarse.

With a shake of his head and a shrug, he got back into his car and drove off giving me a V-sign as he left.

I shouted vainly at his disappearing car, "I still beat you. You fucking PRICK!"

I shouted it with such ferocity it made the neighbours pull back their curtains, curious about all the commotion in the street.

Then he was gone.

I stood alone on the pavement outside 34a Percy Road, left only with my own thoughts and a fuzziness in my head. For a few moments, I stood there, biting my lip, reflecting on what had just happened.

"Fuck you. Fuck you, you bastard. I showed you," I whispered to myself unconvincingly.

I stormed into the house, stumbled up the stairs, and collapsed into bed.

Later, in the depths of my impending hangover, under the safety of my duvet, I realised that he had been angry because he cared—no more, no less. His anger stemmed from fear I would hurt myself, all over a stupid drunken bet.

Two weeks later, Marky left his girlfriend for me. She took it badly by all accounts. It was the best and worst thing he ever did.

Chapter 3

I carefully opened the padded envelope, knowing it was from her. She had been very specific about checking the post. "Check the post. It will tell you what to do," she had said before the call ended.

Panic washed over me. Marky was gone, and I was alone.

Her instructions regarding the police were explicit, delivered in a calm and controlled voice, as if she had done this many times before. The label on the front of the envelope was type written, with a German postmark. I stared at it for what felt like an eternity. Placing it down on the table, I paced around the kitchen, needing another large vodka to calm my nerves.

I hadn't eaten in a week, nor had I slept properly. Brief moments of drink-induced slumber provided only fragmented rest, leaving me neither refreshed nor fully conscious of the world around me. I had stumbled through the week in a perpetual state of confusion and anxious burden. The flat was a mess, but I didn't care. Nothing mattered anymore except finding her.

My emotions oscillated between tears and bouts of hysterical laughter at the absurdity of it all. My baby was gone, and I was lost. Caught in a no-man's land between surrendering to her or raising the alarm. I weighed the consequences but as she had made very clear: she had my baby.

Summoning the courage fuelled by alcohol, I delicately opened the envelope with scissors, still uncertain about involving the police. The contents within made the decision for me. It tumbled out onto the table, wrapped in lace, and covered in linen. With each layer I unravelled, the colour grew progressively darker. A faint tinge in the corner transformed into a rich, deep hue. Finally, I reached the core—an assortment of bloodied wrappings resembling discarded white and red rose petals left under the sun.

Instantly, I recognised what it was. It was a small piece of her finger, cleanly severed, barely half a centimetre. Overwhelmed with horror, I ran from the kitchen and vomited. My hands trembled uncontrollably, and the sheer terror consumed me. Gasping for air and desperate for escape, I barely made it to the bathroom. I missed the toilet bowl and half of my stomach's contents ended up on my top. I remained there for over an hour, replaying the scene in my mind—imagining her being cut, her cries of pain, her desperate pleas for me.

The ordeal threatened to smother me, as if it were a repulsive nightmare from which I would soon awaken. I yearned for a fresh spring morning, with Marky's comforting arm wrapped around me, where none of this would have ever happened.

But reality refused to conform. It was horrifyingly real. I wiped the vomit from my cheeks, took a deep breath, and picked up the flesh—nothing more than a piece of flesh, not my daughter. It was something I needed to dispose of it.

"Rubbish. Rubbish. Rubbish," I chanted repeatedly as I flushed it away.

"I'll go to the police. I need help," I mumbled to myself, the acrid scent of sick lingering in the air. I examined the package and ripped the envelope in half. Inside I discovered a tightly wrapped letter, covered in cling-film.

I began to read. In that moment, my life changed forever. The enormity of the task ahead unfolded before me. Yet, in spite of its contents, a faint glimmer of hope suddenly emerged. A small seed of a plan. A way out. — if I played along. My only hope.

I made my decision.

**

We had been together for six months now. Marky still lived alone in his empty flat after unceremoniously ending things with his Spanish girlfriend. I was taken aback by how ruthlessly and dispassionately he had kicked her out. She had been a complete emotional wreck in the end. But in my eyes, he had a choice, and he chose me. I felt flattered, like any girl would, especially one who had never had a proper boyfriend before. Mum used to say that I scared them off with my high and exacting expectations, and Dad said he was glad about that.

Every day, Marky and I grew closer. We would meet up for lunch, and he would talk about his work, although I didn't really care. I would complain to him about not fitting in with the others in my year, due to my - northerness.

"Sod them," he'd say.

I remember that conversation vividly. We were sitting together between lectures, chatting away. Marky was offering me his best down-to-earth advice.

"You're better than all those fucking upper-class twats. Their parents bought their way into university. You earned your place through honest, working-class, graft. Power to the people," he said, punctuating his little speech with a raised, clenched fist.

I smiled. Marky was a closet communist, which seemed a bit ironic to me, considering he came from a reasonably prosperous suburb of Guildford. But again, Marky was always full of contradictions. He took another drag on his cigarette and extinguished it.

The concourse was bustling with students. Most were milling around in giggling groups, laughing like children in a playground. Others sat quietly, their faces marked by hangovers, collecting their thoughts before lectures, and pondering the question of "why." Some stood alone, with their perfectly organised lecture notes and lack of social skills.

"Thanks. Sometimes I'm not even sure I should be here," I replied.

With that boost to my ego, he leant over and kissed me. It was a lingering, daytime kiss—an inappropriate kiss. If someone else had done it, I would have cringed and looked away. But this kiss was different. It was his, and he was mine. We kissed in broad daylight, in front of everyone. I simply didn't care.

Every day, we grew closer. We weren't officially a couple yet, but we were more than intimate friends. We were oblivious to everyone around us. I would count the hours until I could see him again, and I believed he did the same, or at least that's what I thought. I became breathless when he walked into a room, blushing like an embarrassed schoolgirl. I would fall asleep with thoughts of him and wake up with his image lingering in my mind. Each passing day deepened our emotional connection, developing into a wordless, mutually understood, and unresisting bond.

I remember the day he asked me the question.

It was early January 1986. Marky had let me drive his car to the New Forest. I remember that day distinctly because it was cold, crisp, and snow had fallen for the first time in years. We parked in Lyndhurst and trudged through the crunching, ankle-deep snow to the top of Bolton's Bench—a summit crowned by an ancient oak tree on a gentle, rolling hill. It was early on a Sunday morning, and we were completely alone. I gazed down the hill, observing our intertwined footsteps in the newly fallen snow, which lay as smooth and white as a freshly ironed pillow. Hand in hand, I couldn't distinguish between his steps and mine. They were one and the same.

In silence, we admired the transformed forest—a rolling, gently white-capped woodland, as if adorned with confectionery icing. Despite my efforts, I couldn't hear anything except my own breathing, which billowed in clouds of foggy air in front of me.

"Alice in Wonderland," he repeated, breaking the stillness.

"What?"

"Alice in Wonderland lived here."

"In the forest?"

"No, the girl who inspired Alice lived in Lyndhurst. She's buried in the village."

"Did she have a tiny or a big grave?"

Marky playfully punched my arm.

"You can be a silly cow sometimes."

That's when the giggles erupted, as I continued the joke.

"Did the Mad Hatter attend the funeral? And what about that cat with the big smile?"

"Enough," he replied, trying to stifle his own laughter.

"I try to teach you a bit of culture, and you just take the piss.

Come here."

He leaned down and gave me a gentle kiss. I felt his warm breath on my face, and it felt so good.

Then he asked.

"Do you want to move in with me?"

I knew the question was coming, but I hadn't prepared an answer. I was undecided, not because I didn't want to be with Marky, but for another reason.

I made him wait for a few seconds, which he misinterpreted.

"Sorry, Kirst, if it's too soon. Just think about it," he said.

I reached up and kissed him.

"No, I'd love to, but one condition," I said.

"Sure, what's that?"

"No, sorry, two conditions," I added.

"One: I'm not going to be your cook and cleaner."

"Of course, fifty-fifty," he replied, though I would soon lose that battle.

"...and the other one?"

"I won't sleep in the same bed she slept in. Period," I stated bluntly.

Marky stood there, pondering it for a few moments. Finally, he responded.

"Okay, I'll figure something out."

"Thanks," I said, putting an end to the topic.

With that settled, I waved what I had brought along in front of him.

"It's time to give this baby a go, then?"

"You've been dying to throw it all the way up here, haven't you?"

I nodded sagely and gave him a pursed smile.

For some reason, I had decided to bring the boomerang Dad had given me before I left for university. It was his little joke.

"Here we are, Kirsts. It'll bring you back home to us. I bought it when your mother and I visited Australia last year. Keep it," he had said.

"Thanks, Dad. It's a different kind of leaving present, but thanks."

I remember his eyes becoming moist as he shuffled back into the kitchen.

It was a work of art. I wasn't sure what kind of wood it was made of, but the grain had a deep, rich redness to it. The exquisite painting and varnish was adorned with symbols and images only an Aborigine could understand. Countless hours must have been poured into its creation, a labour of love by a native of the Australian Outback. Or perhaps that was just my imagination, envisioning how things could be rather than how they were. I was like that then. It had probably been made in factory in China somewhere.

I used to hang it from a hook above my bed, a reminder of Mum, Dad, and home. At night, I would lie there, gazing at it as it swayed gently above me like a mobile above a child's crib. Its presence brought warmth and comfort as I drifted off to sleep.

Ever since Dad gave it to me, I had been eager to throw it. I even borrowed a book from the local library on how to make and throw boomerangs, but I returned it mostly unread. It all seemed a bit too complicated for me—stances, wind direction, elevation. However, one piece of advice stuck in my mind: "*Ensure you snap your wrist. This will create spin and uplift, bringing your boomerang safely and securely home.*"

In my mind's eye, I had thrown that boomerang countless times. Each time, it gracefully returned to my hand in one effortless motion. Now, I wanted to make it happen, right in front of my new boyfriend. I knew he would be impressed.

Standing as close to the top of the hill as I could, I assumed what I thought was "the stance." Taking a deep breath, I pulled the boomerang as far back behind me as possible and with one colossal twist of my body, launched it into the air with a grunt.

"Ahhhh...!"

The boomerang soared into the sky, flipping ninety degrees at lightning speed, then descended and grazed the top of Marky's head before skidding to a stop in the snow. He screamed.

"FUCK! Jesus-Fucking-Christ, woman! What are you trying to do? Kill me? You've got the whole fucking New Forest to throw that bloody thing!" he cried, rubbing his head vigorously.

He checked his palm for any blood.

"Oh my God! I'm sorry. Are you alright? Let me see. I didn't mean it. Sorry."

I hurried over to examine the top of his head. It looked grazed, but fortunately, I had narrowly missed scalping him.

"Look, just stand over there," he said, pointing to a spot that was a safe distance away from him. "...and just throw the bloody thing!"

Anger began to well up inside me. I was determined to prove him wrong. I picked up the boomerang and wiped off the snow, along with some of his hair, using the sleeve of my khaki jacket.

One more attempt.

I assumed the position again and launched it into the air. It soared high, disappearing into the distance, and was gone.

I hadn't thrown a boomerang; I had merely thrown a stick.

"Excellent second try," Marky said sarcastically. "...at least you didn't hit me that time.'

"Oh. No. That wasn't supposed to happen," I uttered despondently.

"Don't worry, you got fifty percent of it right. Just not the coming back bit."

I shot him a stare and trudged off to find my boomerang.

We spent the better part of an hour searching for the damn thing. It had landed in a sea of featureless snow and was completely hidden. It would have been easier to find a marble on a pebble beach.

We roamed around in silence, searching, leaving graffiti-like trails in the pristine snow. Marky remained silent, still upset about his head. And I was silent, berating myself for losing the gift Dad had given me. Another reason for my silence was the fear I had about moving in with him. It wasn't because I didn't love him with all my heart; my passion for him grew more intense with each passing day.

No, I was scared because it meant we would be sharing a bed. Despite all my bravado and tomboyishness, I had never slept with a boy before. I had never been promiscuous, but I had also never been in love. But crossing that bridge was something I had to do soon, and I knew Marky was the one. So, I decided it was time to take that step.

Anyway, we never did find that bloody boomerang.

**

She appeared so innocent, sitting there and posing some of the most mundane interview questions I'd ever heard. Surprisingly, she looked much younger than her years. I could detect a flicker of intensity in her eyes, a flame of hatred that Mutti said she had. Her hands trembled visibly.

Each question she asked was met with my well-rehearsed answers. They were received with smiles and scribbles on a piece of paper, which I suspected were more for show than for record-keeping.

"Täuschung," we would call it back home. Deception, you might say.

Something about her appearance unsettled me, but I couldn't quite pinpoint it. It was an eerie feeling, disconcerting to say the least.

As expected, I breezed through the interview effortlessly. My credentials were impeccable. After leaving Heidelberg, I could have chosen any position I wanted. I selected this one partly because I had a task to fulfil, a closure to achieve, for Mutti's sake and my own. I was hesitant about going through with it, but she was adamant. Mutti always got her way.

Now, I just needed to settle in, gain her trust, and then begin.

I still harboured doubts about whether I could go through with it at all. Months before, Mutti had explained everything clearly. She had spelled out exactly what she wanted. At first, her request disgusted me, as it went against all my training and beliefs. But when she reminded me of what she had done, I understood. She needed to be punished; punished for reigniting the flames after all these years. Mutti was very upset when I told her she had contacted me—she was furious, in fact. I had never seen her so enraged. Now, I know why.

We had met at the Mosell Café, just next to the Alte Brücke. It was a warm, humid evening with a languid pace. Tourists meandered back and forth over the old bridge; a medieval cobbled crossing built above the gently flowing Neckar River.

Surrounding us were the usual hordes of tourists, wandering aimlessly as they criss-crossed the Brücke. University students whizzed past on rickety, ill-maintained bicycles, and Heidelberg locals went about their evening routines. I used to be one of those girls, I thought to myself, as I watched a student nonchalantly steer the handlebars with one hand while enjoying an ice cream with the other.

"Have you ever done that, my dear?" Mutti asked, pointing toward the scene in front of us.

A few meters away, a line of tourists patiently waited to insert their heads into the bronze sculpture of a monkey known as the Brückenaffe. It was a magnet for tourists, who would pose with their heads in the animal's empty skull while their amused friends snapped photos.

I chuckled at the thought.

"No, Mutti, I'm too tired after work to engage in tourist activities."

"And too tired to find a good man? A proper man? A man who won't simply pay you?"

I blushed.

"Yes, Mother, I'm exhausted and too preoccupied," I replied.

From the café, we heard the laughter of tourists.

"Stupid tourists. The worst thing they ever did was put that thing there," Mutti muttered, clearly irritated.

"It spoils the beauty of this spot."

We sat in silence for a few moments. I swirled the remnants of my coffee, lost in thought about her request.

"Wie der Vogel des Walds über die Gipfel fliegt, schwingt sich über den Strom, wo er vorbei dir glänzt," Mutti recited, looking up at me with a smile.

"You remembered the poem?" she asked.

"Of course, Mutti," I replied.

She could see the discomfort in my eyes.

"Rebecca, the punishment must fit the crime. In my eyes, this is an appropriate penance to bring closure to the matter. A penance for what she did to your sister," she spoke with a touch of venom, the same tone she always used when discussing such matters.

I sat silently, staring at the riverbank on the opposite side. It appeared serene and peaceful, a sanctuary away from everything.

From the corner of my eye, I could sense them watching, concealed within the crowd yet obvious to both of us.

Mutti sensed my unease.

"They can only watch. Our understanding remains intact," she reassured me.

I smiled at her, although uncertain.

"Yes, Mutti," I obediently replied, "I will do it."

She cupped my face in her hands.

"Rebecca, you have been such a good girl, such a beautiful daughter. This small act will forever remind her of the pain she has caused. It will bring me peace."

"Yes, Mutti," was all I could manage.

Although my mother desired it, it didn't make the act right or justified in my mind. Yet, who was I to judge? My conscience had already become a tainted, impure reflection of the goodness that once resided within me.

**

Of course, I had to get a little tipsy before we went through with it. Not completely drunk, just enough to take the edge off.

I remember that moment so vividly as we left *The Stile* that afternoon. We had spent two hours discussing life over pints of cider and bags of crisps. Both of us knew what was about to happen.

The sky had such a deep blue hue, and the clouds looked overly fluffy as we exited the bar. We walked a bit closer to each other than usual, holding hands as I led him back to my place.

"Dah-dah! And this is where I live!" I announced, standing outside 34a Percy Road.

"Anybody home?" he asked.

Then I remembered.

"You're not allergic to cats or anything, are you?"

"No. Is anyone else here?" he repeated.

A slight blush crept across my cheeks.

"No, Gavin's on a ship somewhere, and Dave is out doing his thing. He won't be back for hours."

"What's he up to?"

"God knows. Everything and nothing, I expect."

I led him into the house. Marky recoiled upon seeing the cats.

"Ohh!"

"Don't ask," I reassured him. "It's a long story. They won't harm you unless you try to steal their food."

"Okay," he said, tiptoeing past them as they shot him angry glances.

One cat, whom I had nicknamed "Scampi," gave him a disapproving scowl.

"Do you want a coffee?" I asked, making an obvious advance that surprised even myself.

"No, thanks," he replied with a smirk.

"Do you want to see my room? There are no cats in there. Well, except for me!"

I pinched the back of my hand as soon as the words left my mouth. Why didn't I just take my knickers off right then and there and get it over with? My only excuse was that I was slightly tipsy, deeply in love, and desperate.

Months later, Marky would tell me that this was the exact moment he had an uncontrollable urge to punch the air with his fist, bring it down rapidly, and shout, "Ka-ching!" But on that day, he simply replied, "Great! I'd love to see your room!"

I do remember noticing his arm twitch though.

I led him upstairs, my breath becoming increasingly panting with each step.

"And here is my room. It's not much, but it's home."

He looked around, and I was worried he wouldn't like it. I had made every effort to spruce it up. I had pinned a large, brand-new *Joy Division* poster on the wall, vacuumed the floor, tidied up all my student clutter and sketches, and most importantly, changed the bedsheets. I had even placed a small flower in a glass on the windowsill, attempting to create an impression of tidy organisation that was far from the truth.

"It looks great, and no cats too," he remarked.

"No cats," I whispered.

"No cats," he repeated.

We stood there, gazing at each other. Marky inched closer.

"I suppose we should just..."

A little closer.

"Well..."

"Relax."

Now his nose brushed against mine, his breath warm on my lips, and his chest pressed against my breasts.

"And get comfortable."

"Without those cats," I added.

A waterfall of silence enveloped us. We were completely disconnected from the world, lost in each other's presence.

He kissed and pressed himself against me. I couldn't take it any longer, and neither could he. We both exploded into a frenzy, hastily undressing each other as if our clothes were on fire. I yanked his t-shirt over his head, momentarily panicking as it got slightly stuck and requiring a vigorous tug. For a split second, I worried it would turn into a comical situation that would ruin the romance.

Fortunately, his t-shirt gave up its little struggle. He removed my cardigan, and I tore off my t-shirt.

We were both breathless, consumed by desire. Marky flipped me around and unclipped my bra, releasing my breasts. Tenderly, he cupped them and kissed the nape of my neck. It was the kind of moment that played out in movies and in my imagination, but never in my real life. "Jesus Christ, Kirstie," I thought. "This is actually happening! To me!"

The rest is a blur of sloppy kisses, exploring uncharted territory, and me gripping turgid parts I had only ever touched in my wildest dreams. I also recall the single bed moving more vigorously than intended, my nails tracing down his bare back as I screamed at the top of my lungs. The room seemed to swirl around us.

Faster and faster he pressed into me.

Then suddenly he coughed loudly and it was over.

I remember feeling wet and warm below. Strangely, I felt both satisfied and robbed at the same time.

We lay there, panting and entwined. I held onto him with my legs wrapped around him like a praying mantis.

I pulled the duvet over his back, creating a little tent, and leant to kiss him. Tiny beads of sweat glistened on his forehead.

"Thanks," I said.

"No, thank you, Miss Kirstie McBride. Cat Woman, extraordinaire!" he replied.

"Miao," I responded, making him giggle.

I said it again because it sounded funny.

We had reached a significant moment together, and there was no turning back. I was hopelessly, stupidly, sickeningly in love with him.

However, that wasn't the main reason why Marky and I would remember that moment.

Oh no, absolutely not!

During one of the most tender moments of our lives, as we shared gentle kisses, with my legs wrapped around the man I loved, bloody Dave Hudson burst into my bedroom.

He tumbled into the room, limbs flailing.

"I won on the horses!" he exclaimed.

I stared at him, dumbfounded.

"I've never won on a horse before! Twenty to one! A mate gave me the tip. A hundred smackers!" he rambled, like the imbecile he was.

Then his brain finally caught up to the situation as he noticed us entwined.

I erupted in fury. It was a good thing Marky was lying on my chest.

"DAVE FUCKING HUDSON, WHY DON'T YOU JUST FUCK OFF OUT OF MY FUCKING ROOM!" I screamed, blasting his pathetic betting slip with my anger-laden spit.

In a panic, Dave thrust the slip in front of me, as if to prove his winnings.

"FUCK... OFF!"

Suddenly terrified, he dropped the slip onto the floor and fled.

"Shut. My. Fucking. DOOR!" I bellowed as he ran out.

Then he scurried back, quickly grabbing his betting slip from the floor before gently closing the door, as if that could make everything better.

Marky's head bobbed up and down on my heaving, sweaty chest as he couldn't contain his laughter.

Meanwhile, I panted with anger rather than lust.

"Does he always do that? Burst into your room?" he asked, his voice muffled against my cleavage.

"Sorry, the guy's a simpleton," I replied.

"Have you ever considered getting a lock for that door?"

He had a point.

After I eventually calmed down, we returned to our mutually affectionate exchange of kisses. I reclined on my back, reflecting on the damp patches, sweaty bodies, and the exchange of fluids that had happened. Suddenly, all inhibitions had evaporated as we caressed each other, becoming one.

"The bed held up well," he grinned.

"Close call, though," I giggled. "I thought we were going to break it."

We would eventually break it, completely. I would have to fabricate a story to tell the landlady about how I accidentally fell on it.

We untangled ourselves.

Then he noticed the scarlet stains on the bedsheets. I nervously tucked my hair behind one ear, attempting to hide my embarrassment.

"Not again. It always happens to me," I said, feigning nonchalance.

"No worries," he replied, kissing my forehead.

Years later, Marky admitted that it was at that moment he truly grasped the significance of it all.

He was such a naive fool.

I still think about him.

Chapter 4

I understood what Mutti wanted, but I still hesitated about the whole idea. I would sway between ignoring her request and it is keeping me awake at night. The task constantly weighed on my mind. But I had made a promise, and I couldn't go back on Mutti. Nobody went back on Mutti.

I couldn't figure out whether it was the entrapment or the act itself that gave me the most anxiety. Maybe it was both. So, I decided to separate the two. If I could accomplish the first, then it would make the second easier, wouldn't it? One night, I resolved to take it halfway, and no further.

I knew the Crown Plaza hotel well. It was just off Bismarck Platz. I had met a few boyfriends there, poor things. That's where I would find who I needed.

That particular night was another balmy one in the city. The streets were filled with the usual mishmash of trams, buses, bicycles, and pedestrians, each managing to navigate without making contact. The city was still alive and only beginning to slow down. I booked a room using an assumed name, paid in cash. Two hundred and thirty Euros was expensive, but that was the going rate. It was high season, and the city was full with tourists.

I'm ashamed to admit that I was excited, even exhilarated about what I was to do.

I showered and shaved. It was still too early to go downstairs. So, I lay naked on the bed and let the cooling evening breeze caress my skin.

I closed my eyes.

From below, I could hear laughter in the street and the sound of a tourist haggling with a taxi driver over a fare. Slowly, I drifted off to sleep, with the city humming to itself below me.

When I awoke, the sun had set. The breeze had turned into a chilly draft, leaving tiny goosebumps on my arms. I stroked my palm across them, tickling myself. I contemplated my task at hand.

Now was the time - time to play.

I slipped into my most exquisite lingerie and then into a beautiful Bastyan's cocktail dress that a boyfriend had bought me. I slid into the garment and adjusted the boned bodice. It was adorned with fine, nude lace. I ran my hands gently over the material. It felt incredible against my skin. Such a thoughtful gift. He had been so sweet. Although, when we broke up, I wasn't so upset as to return his expensive gifts. I'm not that silly. It had been a transaction; no more, no less.

I took a step back, admiring my reflection in the mirror, and smiled. I put on my statement heels. Finally, with a delicate application of scarlet lipstick and minimal foundation to enhance my cheekbones, my preparation for the game was complete. I looked gorgeous, good enough to eat.

I couldn't help but feel a thrilling excitement about the entrapment to come. Was I disgusted at what I had become? Maybe.

I rolled my tongue over my upper lip, catching the light and making the deepest shade of 'Little Red Riding Hood' red, glisten.

"Well, Rebecca, let's go and catch us big bad wolf, shall we?" I whispered.

I ran a finger through my spiralling ginger locks, contemplating.

"Catch a big bad wolf....,"

I grabbed my clutch bag, yet another superficial gift, and headed for the bar.

I knew I would find him there.

**

Entrance is everything. Mutti had always told me that. I strutted with my best super-model walk as I entered the reception area, my heels clicking sharply on the polished marble floor.

I paused to wipe my nose. The powder had hit the spot. In that sweet, transient moment, the sound bounced off the walls, and the colours started speaking to me. The receptionist grinned inanely, and I smiled back at him. I waited for it to pass and then felt the comforting warmth settle in.

The cocktail bar was a dimly lit series of alcoves and meeting spots. It was mostly empty, but I wasn't bothered. I had played this game before. Give men drinks and enough time away from their wives, and they would always seek out, how can I say, "excitement." Crown Plaza was a businessman's hotel, and this was where I had caught most of them.

I picked a quiet, shady alcove, making sure I was still visible, and ordered a small wine.

I waited.

And then, almost on cue, I spotted him.

The poor chap was dressed in a well-fitted brown business suit. His dark tan shoes, buffed to a shine, indicated wealth. He carried a bit more weight than I would have preferred, and despite his relatively young features, his hair was almost white. He seemed around forty-seven, maybe a little older. I could tell he was slightly out of place, unsure of the surroundings and the etiquette of ordering a drink. He looked American or British, I would say British. He downed his beer in almost one go as soon as it arrived. Yes, he was British.

At first, we exchanged just little glances. I would shyly look away, cup, and sip my wine, pretending not to notice. It was a well-practiced tease. Minutes merged into nearly an hour, and I continued sipping my wine. At just the right moment, I would look up to catch his gaze and then look away again.

To be honest, I went on autopilot. I had done this so many times.

As the night wore on, I could feel his eyes burning into me as he grew braver with each glass.

I pulled out my mobile phone and pretended to check it, tapping away into the handset with imaginary texts. I huffed and puffed, making sure he could see my frustration.

His glances turned into stares, poor man.

When I caught his eye, he would turn away, embarrassed at what he was doing, and take another gulp of his drink. Was it the third, the forth maybe? I crossed and uncrossed my legs, ran my hand up and down my calf, and tucked a strand of hair behind my ear. Just as I saw him fidgeting on his barstool and thought he might leave, unable to handle it any longer...

I pounced.

He instantly shrank into his seat as I approached.

I ignored him.

I strode up to the bar, pretending to be a little tipsy, leaned over the counter, and asked the bartender, who was arranging glasses underneath.

"Entschuldigen Sie mich. Mein Handy ist tot. Gibt es ein Telefon in der Nähe?"

The bartender replied, very politely, that there was a phone in the foyer.

Wearing my best frown and disillusioned look, like a child disappointed on Christmas morning for not receiving the desired gift, I turned to him and stood a little closer than he expected.

I let out a little sigh, "Das Leben ist nicht fair?"

He almost fell off his barstool.

There was a moment of silence as he didn't know what to do.

"I'm very sorry. I don't speak German,"

Then he realised what he had said and continued in schoolboy German, "Sprechen... Sie... Englisch?"

"Of course," I replied, putting on my best English accent.

"Oh," I said, "Life's not fair."

"Why?" he asked.

"My friend stood me up. I've been waiting for a bloody hour."

"Oh, I'm sorry. I did notice," he replied.

I sat down next to him, pulling the stool closer, and let out another little pathetic, self-pitying sigh.

"Barman, can I have another glass of wine, please?"

The bartender turned and without a comment, adjusted to my change of language.

"Of course. The same?" he asked.

"Yes, please,"

Then I asked the rhetorical question - the one that always gets them. It would at least tell me how much of a bad boy he was.

"I suppose I'll just have to find some other fun tonight? Or maybe just go to my room all by myself?"

Then he crumbled and asked the bravest question he had ever asked a woman, including his wife, and it had taken him four strong German beers to get there.

"Can... can I get that drink for you?"

He almost blurted out the words, as if he couldn't hold them in any longer.

I paused for a second and kept him hanging.

"Actually, that would be rather nice. Sorry, my name is Samantha. It would be nice to speak English again."

The expression on his face was priceless, a look of wonderment at what was happening.

I could tell he was married. He wasn't wearing a ring, but his appearance gave it away. No man who wasn't married or gay had shirts so neatly pressed. Besides, I could see a faint tan line where his wedding ring had been after he had removed it. Just another sly, deceiving bastard. They all are.

We talked for two hours. He told me his name was Richard, and he was in Heidelberg doing some project for an American multinational. He tried to make his work sound interesting, but it sounded more boring than an accountant's. Yes, that's what he looked like: a pudgy, dull accountant with bad teeth. It was all frightfully tedious, but the rules of the game were simple: look interested in everything they say, laugh whenever they said anything remotely funny, and say "Wow!" whenever they revealed details of their dull, tedious lives.

As the night wore on, I found myself warming to him. There was something quite childlike in his jokes. As I laughed, he would become more confident, helped by the drink. Then at moments, it would all become too much for him, and he'd gaze into the distance, as if remembering something. It was all rather endearing.

I made up a fictitious tale of being a translator for the university. It was a pack of lies, but I spun a good yarn, and he seemed to buy it. Maybe I should have been an actress instead. I found it all so very, very easy. But I was well practiced by now.

As the evening dragged on, as it inevitably did, he loosened up. After many expensive alcoholic drinks he went from being scared shitless, to shy and uncomfortable, then to calm and relaxed, and finally, as always, to cocky and self-confident. As for myself, I moved on to sparkling water, for I had a job to do.

**

"So, that's my story. I'm here to turn a small, unprofitable part of the business around... For that's what I do," he slurred.

"Turn them around," he repeated, clumsily placing the glass onto the counter with a failed attempt at gentleness. It's always interesting to witness the collision between coordination and reality when someone is drunk.

I mustered my best "Oh my God! Aren't you amazing?" and fluttered my eyelashes.

Richard puffed out his chest, falling for the flattery - hook, line, and sinker.

"Amazing. Truly amazing," I reiterated.

"...or close them down," he laughed, before stumbling off to the rest-room.

Fat and stupid. He was exactly what I had hoped for.

When he was out of sight, I quickly slipped something into his drink and flashed a smile at the bartender. He was rather cute, if I remember, but I needed to focussed on the job in hand.

**

"Are you sure?"
"Of course. I'd like to meet them."

"Okay. Next weekend then. We'll drive up and pay them a little visit, stop for Sunday lunch?"

"Sure, I can't wait to see them."

I lay there and stared up at the living room ceiling. Marky could sense my uncertainty. I closed my eyes and felt his kiss on my slightly sweaty forehead and his panting breath on my face.

"It'll be fine."

"Thanks."

"I enjoyed that," he whispered.

"And me," I replied, still keeping my eyes closed.

"You're not very fit, are you? I did all the work. Why don't you go on top sometimes?"

I opened one eye.

"Thanks, and I suppose I sweat too much because I'm a fat lass?" I retorted in my strongest Yorkshire accent.

He burst out laughing.

"No."

I frowned at him.

"We must start these things gently. It's not a race, you know. Besides, a gentleman should do all the work."

"Well, you just lie back and think of Yorkshire then."

"I will, and this lady would like some breakfast in her, umm, sort of bed."

He recognised the sarcasm in my voice.

"I'll get a new bed, promise. Honest."

Marky's solution to my refusal to sleep in her bed was a rather unsatisfactory situation where we both slept on a foam mattress in the living room. It was a bit impractical, but it was surprisingly comfortable in a spongy sort of way. It felt a bit like camping in our own living room.

It was a Sunday morning when he suggested that we visit his parents for the first time. We had just finished making love, which I referred to call an extended cuddle. Marky banging me was an experience I was becoming a bit addicted to. He was getting quite good at it too. As Mum used to say, "It's the quiet ones you've got to watch out for."

So, well, I had to meet his bloody parents in Guildford. I was dreading it. His father was a financial consultant, while my father fixed buses. His parents lived in a large, detached house, while mine had only recently purchased their council house thanks to Maggie.

It felt too soon for me. We had only been living together for six months, but reluctantly I gave in. I was filled with nerves and self-doubt about the whole visit. So a week later, we finally arrived at his house, my stomach in knots and me wearing my best, or rather, only dress.

**

I stood in awe.

"Nice house,"

Fuck, it even had its own private drive.

Marky didn't reply. He seemed a bit on edge as well. It was a spring morning, one of those clear days that signalled the approach of summer.

I remember the visit for several reasons. Firstly, because we drove up in Marky's new car, or rather, a second-hand blue Austin Maestro that his father had bought him. We both thought it was fantastic at the time. In later years, I realised it was a piece of crap, built in the waning days of the '70s. But back then, we thought it was fab.

The other reason I remember the visit was that I made a complete fool of myself.

It also made me realise just how different Marky and I were. This difference would become the foundation of our future troubles. Although I didn't know it at the time. Because I absolutely loved him then, and that clouded everything.

But I went with an open mind. We stood on the doorstep, taking a collective sigh together.

But before Marky could ring the bell, the front door swung

open.

A tall man beamed at me.

"Ah! The girl who ticks all the boxes!" he roared.

I was a bit taken aback.

"I'm sorry?" I replied, before Marky intervened.

"Dad, stop being stupid."

"Kirstie, this is Geoff, my father. Kirstie, Geoff. Geoff, Kirstie."

"Very pleased to meet you," I replied, barely stopping myself from curtsying.

"You said she ticked all the boxes," he bellowed, gesticulating to his son.

"Dad, shut up,"

Geoff was tall and remarkably handsome for his age. His hair was almost snow white. He had the look and mannerisms of a man who had military training and always got what he wanted. I would soon discover that he also had a habit of speaking his mind, even when it wasn't quite appropriate. I warmed to him instantly.

He looked me up and down, as if inspecting a purchase, then boomed with his deep voice,

"Come in! Come in! We're almost ready!"

I was herded into the kitchen to meet Marky's mother, Anne, with Marky trailing behind, clearly embarrassed already.

Anne was a polite and somewhat timid woman. She let her husband's bombastic nature wash over her. Anne seemed practically oblivious to it, or perhaps in denial. She stood in the kitchen, hunched over the worktop, fussing with some pastries, and muttering that the oven was acting up again. Throughout the time I knew Anne, she was constantly apologising for things not being quite right, even though everything was usually always perfect.

She put down her pastry implement and turned to me. I thought she would say hello and offer a warm welcome, but instead...

"It's beef today. But Marky says you're a vegetarian?"

She said the word "vegetarian" as if it were a disease, one that I would eventually be cured of.

"I've got a little nut loaf in the oven," she exclaimed proudly, as if it were her first attempt at such a strange and exotic dish. It was.

"Thanks, that would be lovely," I replied.

Suddenly Marky's father stumbled into the kitchen, wearing a deerstalker hat and a thick Barbour coat he apparently always wore when walking the dogs or going to the pub.

"A vegetarian?!" he bellowed, as if he were about to call the police.

"You're not one of those Greenham Common women, are you? I've seen them on the telly. No bras and everything!"

"Geoffrey, don't be so bloody rude to the young girl, will you?" Anne scolded.

Suddenly, he realised the time. It was one minute to twelve.

"Look, we'll be late!"

Marky had told me about his father's bizarre Sunday routine. At precisely noon, he would go to the local pub and drink solidly for an hour before returning home for Sunday lunch, which had already been laid out by the time he came back through the front door. This ritual was an immovable reference point in his week, as if his routine were laid on steel tracks.

Marky and I dutifully trooped across the road to *The Duke of York* to join Geoff, who was already halfway there. Anne stayed behind to fuss over her pastries, which "weren't quite right again."

As we entered the bar, Geoff's pint was already waiting for him on the counter, as expected. After a flurry of ordering drinks, all of which Geoff insisted on paying for, we spent the next hour drinking, talking, and making idle chitchat.

It started off a bit awkward for me, as I didn't have strong opinions on whether Geoff should buy what would soon be known as a "CD player," or even whether they would catch on. But he seemed keen on the idea, believing that if it had been featured on *Tomorrow's World*, it must be worth considering.

As the drinks flowed, the atmosphere became more relaxed. Marky even began to unwind. I watched him and his father engage in conversation about everything and nothing. They even discussed the merits of new endowment mortgages. I felt strangely at home, despite our differences.

His family seemed to embrace the ethos of enjoying the present moment before it slipped away, with tomorrow being a distant concern. In contrast, my family was built on hard work to keep the wolves from the door. They taught me that for every sunrise, there would be a sunset. My family instilled in me a sense of my place in the world and the importance of a spiritual existence that transcended material wealth. It was something a financial analyst in the '80s, or any decade, simply couldn't or wouldn't understand.

Our families were so different. My family enveloped me in a divine cloak, shaping me with their love and guidance, unseen but deeply felt. His family set him up on a higher pedestal, one he would always never fully meet for them, much to their hidden disappointment.

Looking back, those were truly halcyon days, days that would eventually slip away forever. But at the time, I cherished every single moment with Marky and his strange family.

"Indexation, now that's the key!" Geoff shouted at his son, as if they were several yards away instead of just a few apart.

"...but whatever. You don't want to hear about this. Go tend to that lovely girlfriend of yours."

I could just hear that part, although I wasn't meant to. I felt my cheeks flush slightly as I pretended to pick at my nails, feigning ignorance.

Marky came over, wearing a grin on his face as his father continued his discussion about indexation with the barmaid, whether she wanted to engage or not.

I smiled at him.

"Fancy a game?" he asked, nodding towards the shabby pool table.

"...twenty pence a go."

I pondered it for a moment.

In hindsight, what I should have said was, "No, thanks. I've never played before. You go ahead and play with your dad. I'll watch."

But I didn't.

I wanted so much to please him. So, I agreed to give it a go. How hard could it be?

"Okay. I'll play," I replied.

Huge mistake.

After ten minutes of randomly hitting balls, it became painfully clear that I didn't know one end of the cue from the other. The more Marky watched my futile attempts, the more frustrated I became. Marky skilfully potted balls left, right, and centre, while I could only knock them back and forth in a chaotic, Brownian motion sort of way.

And then it happened.

I would remember it for years.

In a fit of anger, I grasped the cue with both hands and turned to face the cue ball, my face a picture of concentration and determination. In the process, my cue struck three pints of lager on a nearby table, toppling them over like skittles, shattering glass and spilling fizzy beer all over the floor.

I stood there dumbstruck, consumed by embarrassment.

Marky's jaw dropped.

Even the music playing on the jukebox suddenly stopped. Everyone in the bar paused and looked at me. In that split second of awkwardness, I wished the ground would swallow me whole.

Then it happened.

Geoff, bless his soul, leapt off his bar stool, punched the air, and shouted at the top of his lungs.

"Strikeout! That's the way to do it, love!"

I could have hugged him. I started laughing.

"I'm really, really sorry."

Bless him, he hurried over to check that no glass had cut me. In a gentle, sweet manner, he took my hand and led me away from the mayhem I had caused. Marky, on the other hand, did nothing.

I made a mental note to remind him of that later.

"Don't worry! Nobody died, sweetheart. I thought you had my lad on the run for a moment. I saw your plan. Lulling him into a false sense of security... then ca-bam!"

I burst out laughing.

"No, that was just me being rubbish at pool," I replied, still feeling embarrassed.

Then Marky's father did something incredibly sweet. He leant down and whispered in my ear, his voice gentle and kind.

"Don't sell yourself short, my love. That's my one piece of advice for you."

I didn't quite understand what he meant.

"Thank you. I won't," I replied, feeling a bit confused.

It was a piece of advice that would stay with me.

Don't sell yourself short, Kirstie. Ever. Ever.

And it stayed with me, always.

Eventually Geoff walked me back to his house, with Marky following a few steps behind. He had suddenly become quiet; displaying his peculiar behaviour again.

**

Half an hour later, we were all gathered around a Sunday lunch that felt reminiscent of a Christmas dinner. It was a feast unlike any I had seen in years. Even my nut roast turned out decent, although Anne believed it could have been left in the oven a little longer, and her Yorkshires hadn't risen as she had hoped.

"Everybody, please help yourselves. I'm sorry it's a bit of a bun fight," she apologised once again.

I sat in awe, marvelling at the spread of food in front of me.

"Anne, you can only do your best," Geoff replied, attempting to be patronising as he patted her hand. For a moment, I thought she might believe him and burst into tears, but she saw through his wicked, dark humour and smiled.

"Geoffrey, I really need to get a new oven,"

Geoff paid no attention to her comment. She seemed to say it at almost every mealtime. He was already busy digging into his food.

I smiled at Marky, who had cheered up a bit, though something still seemed to be on his mind. I blew him a small kiss, catching Anne's attention. I'm sure she blushed for the first time in years before returning to cutting her meat with determination.

After devouring the largest Yorkshire pudding, I had ever seen, Marky's father finally came up for air.

"So, you're training to be a doctor? How refreshing!" he exclaimed.

"Refreshing?" I questioned.

"Yes, refreshing that my son has finally found somebody sensible, and shall I say, a little less 'Continental,' " he replied.

I didn't say anything. I could see Marky cringe out of the corner of my eye.

"Very emotional, Continentals," Geoff proclaimed, tarring an entire diverse and rich population with one sweeping generalisation.

"I'm from Yorkshire," I retorted, as if it made a difference.

"Excellent. Good English stock, and you've got nice puddings as well," he roared, taking a large gulp from his wineglass as if it were his last drink ever.

"Thanks," I laughed.

"Marvellous puddings," he repeated.

Marky turned crimson with embarrassment. His mother paid no mind and continued sawing at her meat as if it were made of wood, claiming it was still a bit tough and further evidence that the oven needed to be replaced.

The next few hours went swimmingly for me. Geoff told crude jokes, each one more vulgar than the last. These were interspersed with tales of Marky's misspent youth, stories that made him increasingly embarrassed as the afternoon progressed. I thought he might explode and storm off from the dinner table.

After an afternoon of laughter and some of the biggest giggles I had in a while, it was finally time to leave.

Marky stumbled into the car, a bit tipsy, if I remember. He simply couldn't keep up with his father, who, despite drinking like a fish, never appeared drunk.

"You take care now. Have a safe trip back. Come again," Marky's dad said with not sign of intoxication, despite downing at least two bottles of red wine single-handedly.

I thanked them both and gave Anne and Geoff a goodbye kiss before getting back into the new car. I distinctly remember Marky's father hugging me a bit too tightly for my liking and placing his hand on my hip inappropriately, though not so intrusively that it warranted a slap.

Finally, we drove off. As I looked in the rear-view mirror, all I could see was Marky's father waving a small Welsh flag on a stick for no apparent reason, while blowing extravagant kisses.

They were truly lovely.

As we left the driveway and turned the corner, Marky let out the most relieved sigh I had ever heard. His breath, heavy with alcohol, filled the car.

"Wow! That went much better than I expected,"

I chuckled.

"They're nice. Really nice."

"I think they like you, Kirsts," he slurred.

"I like me too. So that's a good thing, isn't it? They've just joined the growing club: The Kirstie McBride Fan Club."

"No, honestly," he said, opening up, likely due to the alcohol. "They can be a bit difficult, especially Dad. He's a bit..."

"...fucking mental," I finished his sentence.

"...well, particular. But if he likes you, then he'll move heaven and earth for you."

"He likes you."

"So much so that he kept gawking at my breasts?"

"Sorry, that's just Dad."

"Your mother is nice, so different from your father."

"A bit scatter-brained," he replied.

"Scatter-brained is nice too. I'm sure I'll be scatter-brained one day, baking cakes in the middle of the night and trying to wash my cats."

Marky didn't respond, which was probably for the best.

We drove in silence, both reflecting on the day. The clouds had rolled in, and rain splattered against the windscreen. We sat listening to the sound of raindrops hitting the glass and the hum of the engine. Finally, we arrived at Hockley lights and waited the usual eternity for them to change.

I looked up at Twyford Down, its grassland shimmering and swaying in the rain shower. Five years later, a motorway would slice through the down in an enormous act of environmental vandalism, which would make my blood boil as the new M3 bulldozed its way to Southampton. But at that time, all I did was sit in the traffic and wonder why Thatcher couldn't sort out that bloody road. It was the 1980s, for Christ's sake.

Then I remembered.

"Oh yes! What *are* all these boxes that I supposedly tick?" I inquired.

Marky burst into laughter, a laugh that turned into a giggle.

"Come on, spill it."

"Do you really want to know?"

"Yes, and to start, how many boxes do I tick?"

"Three," he replied.

"And what are they?"

"Okay, but you asked for it."

"Yes, out with it," I repeated sternly.

"One, you're a redhead."

I shot him a frown.

"I hate to burst your bubble, but it's henna."

"Whatever, it still works for me, cuffs and collars and all that. So, I think you're fibbing."

"And box two?"

"You have a northern accent. Very sexy."

"I'm from York. You should get up to Newcastle."

"And box three?"

He started sniggering again, which only made me angrier.

"And box three?" I pressed, using my headmistress voice.

"And box three," he began, "is that you've got a bloody fantastic pair of tits."

The words practically burst out of his mouth, and he erupted into a fit of laughter.

"Thank you," I replied slowly, secretly pleased by the compliment but unwilling to show it.

Then I realised.

"Yorkshire puddings! Cheeky bugger! Next time I see your bloody dad, I'll give him Yorkshire bloody puddings."

Chapter 5

With a deep, guttural moan, he finally awoke, sounding like a boxer trying to pull himself up off the canvas after a knock-down punch.

"Den...ise?" he croaked, squinting, and looking around the room, his disorientation evident.

I had been sitting and waiting for two hours for my lover-boy to wake up. The flash of my camera phone eventually roused my slumbering beauty. Although I use the term "beauty" loosely here. Stripped down to his boxer shorts and securely bound to the chair with insulation tape, he was far from a pleasant sight. I did take the liberty of brushing his hair for him, bless him, and even planted a little lipstick kiss on his forehead as I deposited his drugged body onto the chair.

During the waiting period, as my little Richard snored away, I meticulously examined the contents of his wallet. Let me stress that I only peeked and replaced everything exactly as I found it. I may be many things, but a thief is not one of them.

Now, I knew almost everything there was to know about him: his home address, email, his phone number. I even caught a glimpse of his poor little wife —a meek, slightly plump woman who appeared to be the epitome of a boring, dull home-maker. He had a small, faded photo of her tucked away in the back of his wallet—how romantic, how sweet, how sad.

In the dim light of the room, I could just make out his silhouette against the city's light. With a groan, my Richard strained to lift his chin from his chest, as if it were the heaviest thing in the world.

Then, in a sudden moment of clarity, he went from dazed and confused to wide-eyed and fully awake. Panic filled his eyes, which widened to the size of saucers.

"UMMMM!" he mumbled through the tape over his mouth.

I stepped out of the darkness, stood before him and placed a finger to my lips.

"Shhh. We don't want to wake everybody, do we, Richard?

You've been a naughty boy," I chided.

"Umm..." he repeated, his voice a bit quieter, looking up at me with sheepish eyes.

I gave the edge of the tape a gentle tug.

"Now, I'm only going to remove this if you promise to behave."

"Do you promise?" I asked.

He didn't reply.

"Oh, by the way, I emailed a few photos somewhere... safe," I added.

He frowned.

I didn't consider it blackmail; rather, it was more of an insurance policy. After all, I had my own professional reputation to protect.

Finally, he understood. He scanned my cocktail dress, now in a crumpled heap on the carpet, then looked back up at me, offering a pathetic nod.

I planted another kiss on his forehead.

"Good boy,"

Then, I ripped the tape from his lips, causing a burning red mark to appear.

"Sorry, Richard, there's never an easy way to do that,"

He started hyperventilating, struggling to find the right words.

"What the FUCK... is going on? What the FUCK is going on?" he yelled.

"Language, Richard! There's no need to be rude,"

He scanned the room, seemingly seeing me for the first time.

"Don't you think I'm dressed this way for a reason?" I said, sweeping my hands theatrically as I stood before him, clad only in my bra, heels, and knickers. "I'm not waiting for a bus, you know? I've been waiting for you to bloody wake up!"

"Sorry?" he stammered.

I shot him an irritated frown.

"Look, one minute you were all over me in the bar downstairs. Then you got completely hammered. I practically had to drag you up here. And just as things were getting a bit close and, well, a bit kinky, you bloody fell asleep!"

The effects of the medication clouded his recollection. He shook his head, attempting to clear his muddled thoughts.

I could see him trying to work it all out, sitting there lost in thought, trying to connect the dots in his mind. Eventually, uncertain, he looked up at me while simultaneously trying to ignore my nakedness.

"Can you take these bloody things off me?" he mumbled, gesturing at his bindings.

I smiled but remained silent, then replied, "Why?"

"Why?" he exclaimed incredulously. "Why? Because I want to fucking LEAVE!"

"Go?"

"Yes."

"But we were just starting to have some fun."

"Let me fucking GO!"

"It would be a shame to stop now. We were just getting started. Besides, I need something from you."

"What?" he asked, irritated.

"A fuck," I stated matter-of-factly.

I watched him flinch at the word. It was all so very British.

I said it again, "A fuck. I need a dirty, filthy hard fuck from you."

I leaned down and gave him a sloppy, wet kiss, forcing my tongue between his lips. He tensed, as they often do, but I persisted, pressing harder. Slowly, he gave in, his protests weakened. As expected, he finally surrendered, relaxed, and became pliant.

I pushed my tongue into his mouth, and slowly he reciprocated. The more I kissed him, the more he devoured me. His defences finally crumbled, and I had him. He was mine.

From his slightly sweating forehead, I traced a wet finger down the bridge of his nose, into the cleft of his chin, and down his chest. Finally, my finger arrived where I wanted it—the growing bulge in his underpants.

He let out a gasp.

I pressed my finger to my lips.

"Shush. Be ever so quiet. We don't want to wake the neighbours, do we?" I whispered.

Richard gently shook his head, obediently following my lead.

Kneeling, I rested my cheek softly on his thigh. He smelled of sweat and cheap hotel soap. I waited a few moments for my Richard to calm down before rubbing my nose and then my palm over his growing problem.

"No... please," he whispered.

I could sense the strain in his voice, the insincerity in his words. But he repeated it again, fainter this time.

I didn't respond and continued to arouse him.

I rubbed and rubbed, and Richard's breathing grew deeper. I released his shaft from the confines of his underpants and wrapped my hand around it. He was practically panting now, his breath the sound of a man who had just run up a flight of stairs.

I glided my hand up and down, slowly stroking back and forth. With each glide of my clenched fist, his protests weakened, and his gasps grew louder. When I could engorge him no further, I straddled him. Slowly, I gently slid down onto him.

"Ahh... Fuck," he gasped.

"Fuck!" he repeated.

"Be gentle," I whispered, but he said nothing.

I kissed his forehead, pressing his trembling head between my breasts as I moved my body up and down.

He made no effort. Perhaps it was the bindings. Regardless, I continued, as a girl has her needs too. Up and down, he slid in and out of me. I moved my fingers down to lend a helping hand.

Faster and faster, I slid up and down on him.

Faster.

Faster.

Faster.

With each thrust, the friction grew less. I felt him swell and pulsate as he started to breathe heavily, in sync with me.

And to be honest, I lost track of time. It could have been minutes, moments, or seconds; I can't recall. In that moment, he was mine. With each downward plunge, the world blurred, and all that mattered was the raw, primal connection.

I squeezed him between my thighs, crushing him against the chair. He let out a little piglet squeal. Richard coughed, grunted, and contorted his face as if in pain.

"Jesus... Fucking Christ!" he exclaimed, followed by a feeble spasm. He spilled inside me, and with a pathetic cry, it was over.

I grasped the back of his neck and pressed his sweaty, scarlet face deeper into my cleavage, rising and falling with my diminishing gasps. I felt him deflating inside me, like a collapsing balloon.

For a few moments, we sat entwined in silence. I brushed his hair down with my hand and kissed his forehead again. He simply stared at the floor as if the worst thing in the world had just happened.

"Thank you, Richard,"

He didn't reply.

"You were very good," I whispered, still trying to catch my breath.

His seed seeped out of me, and he remained silent, hiding himself in my cleavage. I could feel his face trembling, as if he were having a fit.

I pulled myself off him with a wet slurping sound. His juices trickled down my leg.

Then he exploded.

Richard erupted into a cacophony of noise as the fog in his mind finally cleared.

"SORRY, DENISE! I'm so fucking sorry. I LOVE you, Denise!" he screamed, as if these were his final words before the hangman slipped the noose over his head—a verbal protest to all that had just happened. His whole body convulsed, as if he were having a violent seizure.

"I really, really love you. I'm so very, very SORRY," he continued, wrenching at his bindings, rocking the chair back and forth, kicking against the restraints on his feet. He became almost hysterical. Bloodshot eyes, throbbing veins at his temples, his forehead nodding against the backdrop of the Heidelberg night. Each sob was accompanied by gulps of sweaty air, as he ranted like a man possessed.

"Sorry, Denise, I love you... I really do. We can work it out. We can do it for the kids."

"I'm so, so, so SORRY!" he screamed so loudly I feared someone would hear.

I should have tried to calm him down, but all I could do was stand there and smile. He continued sobbing like a toddler who had just been slapped in the supermarket by his angry mother, bawling in protest the injustice of it all.

"Denis, I'm sorry, very sorry. I won't do it again..."

Then, emotionally spent, his sobs subsided into feeble protests, fading into half-mumbled phrases only he could understand.

Finally, he fell silent.

All became quiet.

He looked at me with disgust. I turned away from his glare.

Enough of this, I had things to do.

I cut the restraints and released his ankles, then hoisted him out of the chair. I shifted him onto the bed. He collapsed heavily onto the mattress with a thud. Then I covered him with the duvet, but before I could pat him down, he was fast asleep.

He slept through the night, curled up in a foetal position, facing the wall as if he feared me. I lay next to him, gently stroking his back, contemplating what to do next. I had proven to myself that I was capable, but what would be the next step? Uncertainty still lingered. Nevertheless, this experience helped. It showed me how easy it was.

I drifted off, listening to the sound of his muttering his wife's name in his dreams.

When I awoke, the sun blazed through the gap in the curtains, casting a fiery red glow against the wall and the empty chair in the centre of the room.

He was gone.

I leapt out of bed, searching for any sign or message. There was nothing. No note, no goodbye. He was just another ungrateful bastard, like the others.

Then I noticed the money on the bedside table.

"Ich bin keine Prostituierte,"

The idea repulsed me to my core. That was not who I was.

I kicked the table over.

Mutti had taught me to be a good girl.

"You dirty, filthy little shit!" I screamed.

I stuffed his money into my purse.

Before leaving, I took out my phone and with a few taps, the images were gone, sent to his dearest, lovely Denise.

"Sie haben einiges zu erklären?" I whispered.

He was just another dirty bastard, like they all were.

**

If you are reading this letter, then I assume you have received my little present. Consider it a present to give you encouragement. You have my assurance that she did not suffer when I did it. Cruel, you may say, but it will be a constant reminder of the mistake you made.

She was all I had.

You must pay the price.

These are the rules:

1: Never attempt to contact me, or she will die.

2: Do as I say. I will send further instructions on the tasks you must perform, or she will die.

3: She is mine now. Sign the adoption papers enclosed and take them to the place detailed overleaf. Come alone, or she will die.

4: Never contact her, or she will die.

5: Do not involve the police or anyone else in this matter, or she will die.

Complete all the above, and one day she may be returned.

Best and kindest regards,

Mutti.

At the bottom of the letter, there were tiny, infinitesimal specks of colour, small salmon-coloured stains. Then I realised what they were. I dropped the letter and felt sick again.

It sank in. I was trapped. I had nowhere to go, nobody to turn to. I was completely alone. I remember reading the letter over and over, hoping it would somehow make a difference. I even hid it for a few days, hoping it would disappear, that it was all a terrible mistake. But it wasn't.

I resorted to drinking, attempting to blot it all out.

Eventually I gave in.

The day and time were approaching, and no matter how terrifying it was—terrifying to the point where I was physically sick almost every hour—I knew I had to go on.

Signing the document was the hardest thing I've ever done. I stared at it. It had already been completed with her name and details. All I had to do was sign it and include her birth certificate. It seemed as innocuous as applying for a passport, but it wasn't. I was giving away a child. I was relinquishing a lifetime of future memories that would never come to fruition. I was selling a life that could have been.

My trembling pen left the paper, and I burst into floods of tears, wailing, and wailing. Nobody could hear. I released a wall of hurt, frustration, and emptiness into that empty, filthy kitchen.

Taking a deep breath, I wiped away my tears from my cheeks and chin.

"Calm down, Kirstie," I told myself. "Be brave. Big girl."

I caught a glimpse of myself in the mirror. I looked like a complete mess. I had worn the same clothes for nearly two weeks. My hair was a greasy, lanky tangle. My eyes were bloodshot. I had even started my period and neglected to address it properly. My leggings were stained and reddened. Everything around me, including myself, was unclean and filthy. I hadn't eaten in four days, maybe more, and it showed. My cheeks were drawn and hollow, like an empty coffin. I was a mere shell of the girl I used to be, teetering on the edge, on the verge of collapsing inward. I stood at the precipice, close to falling into a pit of self-pity.

But I didn't.

In a rare moment of clarity, I did what Mum would have told me if she were there.

I pulled myself together.

I fucking pulled myself together.

Mum would have held me, squeezing me tightly until the pain inside became her pain as well. We would have faced this together. But the truth was, I only had myself now. I had to simply forge ahead, alone.

And so, I began.

In that moment, despite the desolation and solitude, the letter ignited a fire within me that would burn for the next thirty years—a fire that provided hope. It also kindled a fire of revenge, an unstoppable force propelling me to uncover what I had done wrong.

Looking back at that moment now, it amazes me that I had the courage to continue. I had lost my husband, and now my daughter. But I was a determined woman. I had no forward plan, only an unwavering belief that she would be returned to me, and a commitment to do anything to make it happen.

Anything.

In that moment, I made an oath that it would be so.

75

I snipped a tiny corner off the stained letter, barely noticeable. I placed it between two slivers of paper, sealed and folded them, then tucked the paper wrapping into the back of my purse. I would carry it with me for three decades.

If I had known the truth, I would have never embarked on the journey.

But at least I was moving forward.

Onward.

I signed the adoption papers. It was done.

Onward, Kirstie, onward.

**

The sun rose over the common, and as it peeped over the crest of the woodland, the autumn-burnished chestnut leaves took on the colour of fresh orange peel. They glowed, signalling the end of summer. I had sat for nearly two hours in the darkness, shivering, waiting.

The only people up at this hour were a few dedicated dog walkers; a group of giggling students stumbling back from town after a night of clubbing, and a drunken homeless man dragging a super-market trolley along. Now they were gone it was silent. So quiet I could hear a faint tinnitus whistling in my eardrums.

Then I saw her—a faint shape of a girl approaching the rubbish bin. I squinted, trying to make out her face, but it was concealed by a scarf. She wore clothes that seemed too big for her.

Then, she veered off.

Perhaps it wasn't her.

But then she stopped, gave a nearly imperceptible shake of her head, turned, and walked back to the bin.

She reached inside — put something in — and retrieved my parcel. Tucking it into her coat, she walked off calmly, heading down The Avenue toward the city centre.

I had an urge to chase after her, to throw her to the ground and pummel her face into a bloody mess. But I restrained myself. It wasn't meant to be. It was too dangerous. I waited until she became a speck in the distance. Looking down, I realised I had pressed my nails so hard into my palm that they were now nearly bleeding.

She began to fade into the distance.

Then I snapped, for some reason. In a wave of anger, I stumbled out of the bushes and raced after her. Clumsily, sprinting in my Doc Martens, I made loud and ungainly steps in pursuit. She turned. I half expected her to run away. But she didn't. She calmly turned around and continued walking.

Then I struck her.

I hit her and her body crumpled. She let out a grunt as the breath was knocked out of her lungs. Now panting like a hunted animal, I span her around and pinned her under my weight. I tore off her scarf and just as I was about to swing my fist back to shatter her face into a bloody pulp...

I stopped. I froze.

She looked up at me with the calmest, coldest expression I had ever seen. There was no emotion—just a cold, empty stare. Her eyes, as blue as cut gemstones, locked with mine for a split second. Time seemed to trip. I stared back.

She appeared to be around the same age as me, maybe a year or two younger. Her face was thin, and her cheeks slightly hollow. I didn't know what I was expecting, but she looked so young, so incredibly young.

I was the first to blink. I turned away.

Then I completely lost control. Even after all these years, I remember it vividly. A furnace of hatred boiled over. I spat into her face, releasing every ounce of fury that churned in the pit of my stomach. I had never spat at anyone before, but I did it then, and I meant every single drop of it.

"You fucking... BITCH! WHAT ARE YOU DOING TO ME? WHAT HAVE I...EVER DONE TO YOU?"

She lay on the ground, completely unfazed, her face splattered with my spittle.

"Alles," she replied calmly.

"You have done everything," she continued.

I didn't understand.

"Du bist Baby wird sterben," she uttered.

I stared at her, my breath blowing heavy gusts of moisture into her face. She paid no attention and replied, "Your baby will die."

She spoke the words with complete certainty, as if there were no doubt.

Momentarily our stares locked together.

Cupping my clenched fist in my lap, I glared at her in silence.

Then the spell was broken.

Bits of twigs and leaves clung to my hair. I shook them free and pulled myself off her.

Turning, I stumbled forward, confused, my heart pounding in my chest. I had to get way.

I reached the bin, retrieved the letter, tucked it into my back pocket, and turned around.

But, she was gone.

I felt numb as I walked home, like a zombie, lost in my own world of worry.

I crossed the common and made my way back to my empty, dirty flat.

An hour later, I knew what my first task would be.

Chapter 6

"April 5th, that's Grand National Day!"

Marky's father was furious that we were getting married on the biggest day in the horse-racing calendar. Geoff was an obsessive gambler. All investment bankers probably are. Horse racing was his passion. As for me, I never saw the fascination myself. My interest in horses was more inclined towards show jumping. However, I hadn't been on a horse in years, not since I busted my ankle attempting a three-stride jump in two, falling off and paying the price. So, when we said we were tying the knot on that very Saturday, the celebrations were marred by Geoff throwing a tiny fit.

"Are you sure?"

"Sorry, the Registry Office is now booked. It was the only Saturday slot still available in April," Marky replied.

"Yes, but it's bloody National Day!"

"Geoffrey, stop being so bloody rude. They can get married when and wherever they like. You can catch the race highlights in the evening."

"Catch the highlights!" Geoff replied, incredulous at the very thought of it.

"Don't worry, we'll set up a TV at the reception. You can watch it there. We'll be done with the speeches by then," I interjected, attempting to calm the stormy waters.

If the 'when' was an issue, the 'where' was also a bone of contention. Both of us had less money than a church mouse at the end of the month. We agreed it would be a quick ceremony at the Southampton Registrar's Office, and it was indeed quick. I remember thinking, this should be my big day, not my big 'moment'. After that, we all headed to a local, shabby Scout hut for the reception. I recall the place smelling of bleach and unwashed schoolboys. The function was a simple affair, consisting of an open bar, a cold buffet, and a collective viewing of The Grand National. His father insisted on it, so I finally relented.

Every expense was spared, but we didn't care. We loved each

other, then.

I vividly remember Marky's father taking charge of the proceedings during the race. He insisted that the television sound be turned off whilst he performed the commentary himself using the karaoke setup while standing on a chair and waving a copy of *The Racing Post* furiously.

The day is etched in my memory. Most of all, I remember the laughter. It was strange to see my family and his family together. At first, Dad looked a bit out of place and uneasy, but after the drink started flowing, which Geoff insisting on paying, the class divide soon crumbled. It was as if they had known each other for years.

Marky's best man, Malik, set the tone of the afternoon with the rudest speech I d ever heard. It was truly shocking. I remember Marky cringing.

"So, I asked Marky, why was he looking forward to marrying his fragrant bride? And do you know what his answer was?"

I remember the entire room staring in anticipation at what Malik was going to say, smiles starting to form on everyone's faces, and glasses held tightly in expectation as the hall fell silent.

"Well, he said it would now be brilliant. Brilliant, as he could finally send those Polaroid snaps of Kirstie off. Off to Readers' Wives!"

I remember everyone exploding with laughter, especially Geoff, who I thought was going to stop breathing, and Mum suddenly going ashen faced, while Marky buried his forehead in his hands, wishing the teasing would stop. Which it didn't.

I remember his best man being so lovely.

Malik was the most thoughtful, kindest person I've ever met. I remember him getting really worked up about us not having a honeymoon. We were just going back to our tiny flat in Highfield after the wedding, as if it were just the end of another day. It didn't bother me in the slightest, but he kept going on about it.

To be honest, it was a bit strange being the centre of attention. I'm usually not unless I've done something extraordinarily embarrassing. But as the day wore on and the heartfelt wishes became more sentimental, I loved it. I truly did.

After the speeches concluded, the trestle tables were folded away, and the chairs were stacked in a leaning tower at the back of the hall. The Scout hut was transformed into an '80s school disco, thanks to Pete and his spinning platter of hits, booked courtesy of Dave. It was his wedding gift, which was kind.

By ten o'clock, the disco was in full swing, with my tipsy relatives dancing poorly and tripping over themselves. I remember Dad taking an unnatural interest in one of Marky's eccentric aunts, which was quite amusing. The air pulsated with '80s pop. DJ Pete had even hung a glitter ball from the ceiling. I recall sitting at the back of the hall next to Marky, reflecting on the fantastic, beautiful, happy day we had both experienced.

**

"So, Mrs. Bowen-Wright, how was your wedding day?"
I leant over and kissed him.
"Lovely, absolutely lovely. Thank-you."
"For what?" he asked.
"Everything,"
He gave me a little shy smile, the smile of a man who knew how lucky he was.
"Drink?"
"No thanks, my tummy's a bit iffy."
Marky looked at me, disbelieving.
"Never thought you'd miss a piss-up."
"I'm a married woman now. I have a reputation to uphold."
Malik stumbled over, clearly tipsy.
He had traces of red wine on his big bushy moustache and was barely managing to hold his glass steadily.
"Great speech, mate," Marky said.
"It was the least I could do. Although I toned it down. Took out

the episode about the pineapple rings."

"Pineapple rings? What's that about?" I asked, but Marky hurriedly redirected the conversation, clearly agitated.

"Never mind. I'll tell you one day, if you're a good girl."

Malik winked at me.

"What this naughty boy can't do with a small tin of pineapple rings isn't worth knowing about."

Marky turned beetroot red and sniggered.

Suddenly Malik stood upright and almost saluted. He toasted us with one hand and presented me with an envelope from his back pocket with the other, offering it to me with a little flourish.

"It's nothing, but enjoy it. It's on me."

I opened the envelope. It contained a booking for a night in a local hotel and a weekend in Devon.

"It's not much, just a B&B. I know a farmer in Barnstaple. It'll be a little getaway for both of you."

"Oh, Malik, that's so sweet."

I think he even blushed when I kissed him before he swaggered off to the dance floor, his tall, gangly frame making awkward movements that both scared and amazed my family in equal measure.

"He really is lovely, isn't he?"

Marky turned to me.

"Don't you mean 'a lovey'?"

I frowned at him. "What, Malik, gay?"

"Well, all I can say is his trousers are a bit tight, and there's a bit of Freddie Mercury about him at times. But he's my best mate and all I've got."

There was a moment of silence.

"You've got me, Marky. I'm your best mate now."

Marky didn't say anything, and at that moment when I was going to tell him, I didn't.

"Your father seems to be enjoying himself," he said, changing the subject.

I laughed at the scene playing out in front of us. Dad was now dancing alone on the dance floor. I had never seen him dance before, and I wasn't sure if I was really seeing it then.

"Come on, let's go outside, get some fresh air."

Marky pulled me into the cooling night air. The sky was pitch, and stars shone down like pinpricks of light through a jet-black cloth. We walked over to the deserted children's playground next to the Scout hut. All we could hear was the thumping beat of music coming from inside, occasionally interrupted by episodes of raucous laughter.

I sat down on the seat of a child's swing, realizing as I did so that my bum was a bit too big to fit comfortably. I rocked back and forth, lifting my feet to prevent my heels from scuffing the ground. Marky smiled at me, smirking at his wife in her wedding dress, wedged in a seat meant for a five-year-old.

"They should make adult versions of these. I miss doing this. Why should children have all the fun? Give me a push?"

He stood behind me, held me by the shoulders, and gave me a gentle push. I swung back and forth.

I could feel his palm pressing into the space between my shoulder blades as he rocked me.

We said nothing.

Then I broke the silence.

"You said 'for richer and poorer' today. Did you mean it? For always?"

My voice came out almost as a whisper, perhaps because I feared the answer.

"For always," Marky replied, but the reply seemed slightly delayed to me, or perhaps it was just my imagination.

And I still hadn't told him.

"Come on, let's go back inside. They'll think we've run off," I announced and extricated my backside from the plastic seat with a firm tug. The seat had left an imprint on my bottom. I brushed away the impression before Marky could see.

"Or maybe we've just sneaked off for a bit of hanky-panky?"

"Marky, is that all you think about?"

"With you, yes," he replied. At least he was honest.

Hand in hand, we stumbled back to the reception, to the pounding beat of Pat Benatar's "*Love is a Battlefield*" as we approached. Looking back now, it was all quite ironic.

**

"Why won't that bloody fucking cow shut the fuck up!" It was three in the morning, and we were both still awake. Marky pushed his head under the goose-feather pillow, attempting to drown out the baying sound. It didn't work. I knew. I had just tried it.

He let out a gasp, pulled his head out from under the pillow, twisted around, and collapsed onto it. It was the final act of surrender, the surrender of a man now convinced of the inevitability of getting absolutely no sleep that night. The animal had won.

He let out a huge, deflated sigh. "It's not a cow anyway. It's a bull, and he's calling for his girlfriend."

Marky turned and gave me a disbelieving look. "You're a bloody vet now, as well as a wannabe doctor?"

"I know everything, don't I?" I teased. "Besides, I did consider studying Animal Science at one point."

"Why didn't you?"

"I realised I didn't like animals that much, except horses, of course."

He grunted in disapproval. He wasn't happy. Marky valued his sleep, and he was probably exhausted after our activities. I just lay there, contented, feeling the damp patch spread beneath me.

"Do you want to swap to my side?" I asked.

"No. Look, it's your mess, deal with it."

"Charming. It's your mess inside me," I replied.

He didn't say anything.

"Look, I'm your new wife. You have to do everything I say now."

He didn't respond but changed the subject.

"I'll bloody kill Malik when I see him."

"Look, it's a working dairy farm. What do you expect?"

He didn't know how to reply. Besides, the whole weekend was free, so we couldn't really complain.

I snuggled back under the duvet. The down-filled mattress must have been a foot thick, and we sank so deep into it that we could hardly move. With the old-fashioned duvet covering us, it felt like being wrapped in a big, cosy, comforting jumper. The bed was a Victorian brass-framed contraption, reminiscent of *Bedknobs and Broomsticks*. It made an irritating creaking sound as we rocked back and forth, which we had done frequently that night. But it didn't matter. The house was empty, and the only one who could hear us making love was Mr. Bull outside. Perhaps that was why he had been bellowing.

It really was a peculiar place. The cavernous house hadn't been lived in for years. When we walked in, it smelled stale and musty, and the decor was a throwback to another time. Though it was relatively clean, we spent the first hour catching bluebottles that were trapped inside, which Marky found appalling.

The afternoon we arrived, it was a gorgeous spring morning that hinted at the coming summer. The air smelled of nature, new growth, and, when we finally reached the farm, cow manure. It all came as a bit of a surprise to my new husband. I had spent a lot of time on farms, riding horses and such, but for him, it was a complete culture shock.

The farmer's wife, Trudy, was very friendly. She showed us around the farm and made us feel welcome. She had the ruddy face of a forty-year-old who had spent most of her life outdoors. Her skin was slightly weathered, but her bubbly personality took a decade off her age, especially when she smiled, which she did a lot. She looked like a woman who had a million tasks to perform just to get through the day.

I remember her showing Marky how to start the wood stove, the only source of heating in the house. He looked at her as if she were asking him to split the atom. He had no idea where to start.

I could almost sense her tutting at him, seeing him as a pathetic urban individual. Anyway, I got the fire going, and soon we had a warm house that smelled of burning oak, dispelling the dampness.

"Stupid," I whispered to myself in the darkness, reflecting on it.

He heard me. "Stupid?"

"You've never lit a fire before?" I asked.

He was silent for a moment, then replied, "No, we have electricity in Surrey. It's very popular, apparently."

Then we both realised the beast outside had stopped bellowing. Perhaps, just perhaps?

But no, he started again, continuing his nocturnal rendition of personal bovine sorrow. Marky huffed to himself.

I lay there in bed, staring at the ceiling, trying to block out the sound of Mr. Lonely Bull from my mind. I decided it was time to tell him.

I took a deep breath and spoke the words I had rehearsed a hundred times in my head.

"I'm pregnant."

I sensed him tense a little under the duvet.

A few moments of silence, then he raised himself up as best he could.

"Jesus, what a great time to tell me! On our honeymoon? Perfect timing, huh?"

Suddenly, he wasn't focused on the bull, who had now paused for a breather.

"You started it," I scolded him.

I was terrified.

I wanted him to share my happiness. The joy and excitement inside me were bubbling over, an ecstasy I could hardly contain. I was going to be a mother, a mummy! I wanted to shout it at the top of my lungs. I wanted him to feel the same.

And he did.

He pulled the duvet over us like a tent, turned around to face me, and still stuck in the quicksand of the mattress, twisted himself like a seal on a beach trying to get back to the sea.

My husband held my beaming face between his hands and kissed the end of my nose, then my lips.

"This is fantastic! A bit scary, but fantastic. Fan-bloody-tastic!"

I nearly exploded with joy. I didn't know where it all came from, but it felt limitless.

"How many weeks are you?" he asked.

"Ten, I think," I gushed.

"Wow! Fuck, I'm gonna be a dad!"

"Yep."

"And I'm going to be a mummy," I added.

He took a deep breath as he absorbed it all. "Do you think your tits will get much bigger?"

For that, he received the biggest jab in the ribs I had ever given him. In fact, I was a bit scared I might have broken one.

"Ahh..! Jesus Christ, only joking!"

"Sorry. Sorry."

When he finally calmed down, we wrapped ourselves around each other in an inseparable moment of love. I imagined our tiny baby's heart silently beating between us.

Sadly, looking back now, I took it all in and believed everything he said, that little shithead.

But I just fucking loved him to death back then.

**

"Wake up! Wake up!"

It felt like the crack of dawn, though it wasn't, when Trudy pounded on the front door so hard, I thought she might shatter the glass.

"Shit."

Marky was fast asleep. All sorts of nightmares raced through my mind in that split-second. Was Dad dead? Was Mum dead? The mere thought sent me into a panic.

I quickly dressed, nearly tripping down the stairs as I struggled with my own knickers.

Perhaps there was an emergency—a fire or something worse?

No. It was just Trudy being Trudy—never subtle, never understated.

She continued hammering on the windowpane.

Breathless, I stood at the door. I was sweaty and looked a mess.

I opened the door, expecting the worst.

"Do you want to come and see the lambs in top field?" she said, completely oblivious to my dishevelled state.

I burst out laughing.

I had only heard the term top field, on *The Archers* or was it *Emmerdale Farm*? It was hilarious.

Trudy took no notice.

She asked with a tone that made it sound like she was offering us a priceless gift that wasn't available every day of the week.

"Well?"

"Yes, that would be great. Is it far? We didn't bring any wellies."

She gave me one of her big smiles.

"No worries. I'll take you up in the Landy."

"Thanks."

Then she stomped off to attend to another task, calling back to me, "See you outside the barn in a bit."

I raced upstairs to share the news.

"Marky! We're going farming!"

He grunted from beneath the duvet.

I yanked the bedding off him and threw open the curtains. Spring sunlight flooded into the room. He curled up in a ball, desperately clutching at the bed linen.

"Get off! Give it back to me," he protested.

I had no sympathy for him. There was another reason he hadn't slept—a reason that wasn't the bull. It was his bloody dick.

"Look, I'm going to be the farmer's wife, and you're going to be my ruddy-cheeked farmer husband. If you behave, you might earn a roll in the hay later."

This remark sparked a positive response, and he unravelled

himself from the bedding like a bear waking from hibernation, planting his feet on the cold floor with a grunt.

Success.

An hour later, we were bouncing around in a ten-year-old Land-Rover Defender that reeked of sheep and their shit.

"The season's nearly over. Some of 'em are quite big now, ready for slaughter," she shouted back to us.

Marky stared at her wide-eyed. Holding onto his seat as the vehicle jolted beneath him, he reminded me of someone trying a mechanical bull or the first time.

Top Field was on a forty-five-degree incline, and as the Land-Rover struggled up the bumpy, slippery grass, I was convinced it would topple over, sending us all tumbling to our deaths. But it clung to the hillside as if glued on. I had never been in a Land-Rover before, but after that experience, I knew I wanted one someday, no question. Much later, I would regret that ambition, big time.

"It really is a wonderful sight, birth..." Trudy said, more to herself as she navigated onward and upward, oblivious to our fear and panic in the back seats.

"Nature gives and takes in all her majestic glory," she shouted back, as we grew increasingly seasick. Judging from Marky's expression, I thought he might throw up.

Suddenly, we lurched to an unsteady stop, almost causing us to be flung out of the vehicle.

We stood, catching our breath in the morning light.

Trudy was right—the scene before us was spectacular. The trees seemed greener, the grass lusher and more succulent on that morning. Seeing the lambs leaping around with their mothers on spring-loaded legs made me feel warm and fuzzy inside. And for some inexplicable reason—perhaps the desire to shout it to the world—I blurted it out.

"I'm having a baby too!"

Trudy's face broke into the biggest smile I had ever seen.

"My, I thought you two just got married last week."

I knew I was blushing. I could feel my cheeks burning, as if set on fire.

"Yes, we're in a race to populate the world single-handedly," Marky sarcastically muttered to himself.

Trudy frowned at him.

"Good on both of you. Good on you," she proclaimed.

We both shifted uneasily, unsure of the appropriate response in such a situation.

"Good on you," she repeated, as if it were the best news she would hear all week.

"Thanks," I replied, still unsure of what to say.

"It was a joint effort," Marky quipped.

Trudy paid no attention.

"Me and my husband, Brian, tried very hard, I can tell you, but it just wasn't meant to be," she continued. She then let out an almost imperceptible sigh, but I caught it—a faint release of breath that betrayed heartache, a pain suppressed.

"Now, you make sure you look after her when she's born. Hold that little one close to your hearts and never let her go."

"Or him?" Marky asked, slightly perturbed by the possibility of a girl.

"No, it's a girl, alright," she drawled.

"I do know about things like these," she replied prophetically.

We didn't say a word.

"If I'm wrong, you can stay here next summer for free."

Then she nodded to herself as if closing the matter, before exclaiming, "Pick one."

"Sorry?"

"Pick a lamb, and I'll have the little one culled and gutted straight away before you leave. It'll be my little gift to you."

"Thanks," I said, a bit taken aback.

Marky didn't say anything but turned pale and gulped.

Yes, he really was a big wuss. A big, cowardly, ungrateful, pathetic wuss who got what he deserved.

Chapter 7

5 Years Later

"How do you deal with the hopelessness of it all?" he asked, his words accusatory.

I heard him, but my gaze remained fixed on the deserted street outside—or what passed for a street. The pitted road, coloured a rusty red, had been parched dry by the relentless African sun, turning it into a sterile powder. I could make out patches of ruddy dirt where their blood had seeped into the soil just a week before. The dust swirled back and forth, erasing all evidence as if the horrors had never occurred. Their bodies were now mere decaying slabs of hacked flesh, stacked in a dilapidated mortuary down a side street that reeked of rotting meat—a mortuary ill-equipped to handle so many. The Rwandan sky beat down upon its corrugated roof, slowly cooking the dismembered remains within.

"Kirstie, how do you manage to carry on in this abyss of fucking misery?"

Gus's voice cut through my thoughts. He was the best nurse I had worked with during my three years with Médecins Sans Frontières. Together, we had witnessed the ravages of war in almost every part of the world—but nowhere was as bad as this.

I turned to face him. He looked drained, worn down by it all.

"Are you okay?"

"Sure, sorry. Got a job to do and all that," he replied softly, wiping his dirty, ginger locks back from his face. He gazed back at the ground, seemingly in another world.

"I know... we're all trying our best," I said, attempting to provide solace, but he wasn't listening.

"You didn't answer my question," he replied, his gaze still fixed on the spot on the ground.

"How do you cope with it?"

"Because I have to," I responded simply, leaving unsaid the

91

reason behind my resilience. Because of her, there was always still hope.

We had both witnessed things that disgusted us to our core—sights of heart-wrenching cruelty that threatened to stain our very souls—things that seemed conjured up by the devil himself. But we pressed on. It was our duty, the oath we had taken, and the promise we had made.

Yet, this was the most horrifying place we had ever been.

"It's genocide," he stated matter-of-factly.

"I know, but let's be careful with our words. We have work to do," I cautioned, trying to redirect his focus.

"I have a really bad feeling about this one, K," Gus said, absent-mindedly scratching his two-week-old beard.

He lifted his gaze from the ground and locked eyes with me. I could see the dampness in his eyes.

"Like, we might not make it out."

His words shook me. If Gus, usually unshakable, was affected by the situation, it meant things were dire.

But we had to find a way out. I had a duty to fulfil. It was the only way forward.

We fell silent, sharing the weight of unspoken fears.

Then, the doors opened slowly, and she entered the room with a gentle grace, as if careful not to disrupt anything.

"Doctor? She's speaking,"

Hard-wired to serve, to walk over burning coals for others, Gus snapped out of his worries and beamed at me.

"Thank God for small mercies. I thought we had lost her."

**

Sometimes as a doctor, you see things that disgust you, inflame you, anger you, and sometimes you just witness things that make you want to weep. But you don't. You carry on, wearing the cloak of the job you must do. This was one of those moments.

She lay on the bed, propped up with all the pillows we could find. Even they weren't enough to give her support. The cushions had collapsed around her, almost swallowing her slight frame.

I'd raised the bed sheets above her lower abdomen, as not to touch the bleeding. The drip I'd secured, with the last of the saline, was all the only thing that was keeping her alive. She was just a shell of a girl, a broken eviscerated ghost of a girl, but one who just kept going. How? I didn't know. I just couldn't figure it out. But she did.

"Precious?"

I approached her bedside, almost whispering the word. I still didn't even know her real name.

I leant down and blew against her grazed cheeks, as if my gentle warm breath would make it all better.

"Can you hear me?"

Nothing.

Then she forced her eye open and looked up at me. The other was gone. Wrapped in second-hand wispy gauge and the only swaddling I could find, it oozed blood. But it was the best we could do.

"Hello Sweetie."

Then she smiled. She fucking smiled after all she had been through. She bloody, fucking smiled.

We had picked her up after the soldiers had left. It was just luck we had found her sheltering in the back of the church, hiding in a cupboard under the crypt, shivering from the chill of the night and from the fear.

Since we had looked after her she hadn't spoken a single word; shell-shocked from what she had witnessed. No, not witnessed. Shell-shocked from what they had done to her.

"What's your name?" I asked.

After an eternity of silence, she finally spoke. She spoke as if it was the hardest thing in the world. She spoke with almost silent words, as if they were all secrets.

"She says her name is Uwimana.", Muteteli translated in faltering steps.

"Hello Uwimana. My name is Kirstie and I'm a doctor. I'm here to help you."

She looked up with a very faint flicker in her eye.

"How old is she and how far on?" I asked.

On conveying the information, I could tell Muteteli, was shocked, shocked, and ashamed, as she was a Hutu as well.

They talked in their own tongue, as the old lady pulled the words from her.

Muteteli turned to us.

"She is thirteen years old, and two months into her pregnancy."

"She was raped by the Hutus," she added as an aside.

She looked older. But this didn't surprise me in the slightest. I'd have been more shocked if it wasn't true. I'd examined the poor child as I unwrapped her from her blood-soaked, shredded cloths when we found her. Every part of her lower body had been whipped and lacerated. Her genitals had been mutilated long ago and were now but disfigured, hardened lobes. She had trouble passing water and would wince at the pain and effort of it, as if she was peeing bleach.

The girl had the body of a bruised, lost soul; one that meant nothing to her perpetrators. She was just a mere bug to them.

"Uwimana, we need to know what happened. Tell us. The world needs to know."

Then she spoke in very broken English.

"Does...does the world care?"

I didn't have an answer to that and felt ashamed.

Gus, sat down next to her. She was so light and frail that her body fell towards him, and in that gentle reassuring way he had, he stroked her hair, moving it away from her eye.

"Uwimana, it's going to be okay."

She turned and looked up at him, knowing he was lying.

"What happened babes? Tell us?" he continued in his soft, comforting South African drawl.

I saw her face become angry as she remembered. Then she

pulled the sheets up under her chin and her face became as frightened as a small child's in an empty house. With a clenched anger in her voice, she told us through the words of the old lady.

"They told us to go to the church, all of us. Nobody would hurt us in the church. When we got there the old people were sad and crying. I didn't know what was happening. I clung to my mother. I was scared after what happened last time."

"And your father, where was he?"

"That was the last time, "she replied coldly, as if I was stupid.

"The army came and others. They got out of trucks. We could hear them outside, the muttering of voices that got louder. I thought they were going to help us, but the old people started to cry again, and the children wandered around confused and hungry."

I could see she was struggling getting the words out.

"Then they came. Came with axes, and knives and machetes."

I bit my lip. I nearly couldn't take it anymore.

"And they cut us, cut all to death. The babies, the children, everyone."

"They were our neighbours, "she said in words that faded into the silent end of a whisper.

"They were our neighbours," she repeated.

I stood affixed to the floor as the Rwandan sun sank behind the dirty blinds of the room, painting Uwimana's face an ember red.

"How many?" Gus asked.

She stared at him.

"I am only child and cannot count such numbers."

All of us adults suddenly felt the collective weight of guilt on our shoulders as she said the words. There was sorrow in the old woman's eyes.

I paused before continuing.

"How did you survive?"

Then she looked up and answered with maturity older than her years.

"I survived? "

"Sorry." I whispered.

95

I could see she was shivering. Gus wrapped the remaining blanket we had over her, and she continued.

"I hid under the bodies. They thought I was dead. I kept still."

Then she said nothing for a few seconds.

"At night the animals came and fed on the bodies. Some were still groaning. In the day the birds picked out their eyes. But I kept ever so still, so still and thought of my mother."

Then she pointed to her bandaged eye.

"The rook did this to me, but I bashed him away, and ran into the church, when they didn't see me. Before the rook could tell them."

We all stood there in silence. All I could hear was the sound of the whirring fan-heater and my panting breath.

In a second caught in time I was torn between two worlds: one to run away and another to do something, to help. In that moment, I chose.

"Can you both get me some morphine from the bag, and find another blanket?" I snapped.

Obediently both left the room.

I sat down next to her and held my palm against her cheek. I didn't say a word, but didn't need to, she knew.

I drew the syringe before anybody could see or find out.

"Uwimana, I'm going to give you something to help you sleep and to help your pain go away."

She didn't understand.

I pressed the contents into the drip-valve. It mixed with the saline in a one-way vortex, and suddenly she became as limp as a rag.

I crept back out, feeling guilty and ashamed. I remember the elderly woman was in tears. Even I became contaminated by it all. I blamed her, the dirty Hutu bitch. Which was so wrong, because that's how it all starts, prejudice.

"Drink?"

I took a swig of whisky from the plastic bottle and passed it back to Gus.

He took it and gulped down the liquor.

"I'm as empty as a hole," he replied, labouring over the words. We both sat on our camp beds, gazing at the floor, feeling punch-drunk.

"When do we make a dash for the border?"

"Not tonight," I said flatly. "There are too many troops around."

"We could leave her behind?"

As the words left his mouth, I could tell from his expression that he knew how wrong they were.

"Sorry," he replied and took another gulp from the bottle.

"We'll wait it out a few days," he could sense my uncertainty in my voice. "We'll make a run for Zaire and the refugee camp. But only when it's safe."

Then I said it. "I think we're being followed."

Gus didn't say anything.

"Okay. You're in charge," he wearily apologised and continued staring at the floor.

"Sorry," I replied. "But I need to think of everyone."

He nodded, looked up, and blew me a kiss.

That night, we slept clothed in each other's arms, against protocol. We slept together to keep warm, but also because we were both so bloody scared and to be honest, I was falling in love with him.

After a few hours, I could hear Uwimana softly sobbing in the room next door. There was nothing I could do. Maybe I had helped her, or maybe not. Only God would judge me. I fell asleep, thinking about where my daughter would be, as I did every night.

When I lost Rebecca, I effectively ran away. I broke the news to my devastated parents, shocked that I had given away their only granddaughter. Mum cried buckets on the phone. Dad snatched the phone from her and, for the first time in my life, spoke to me harshly, confused, and angry.

"What the bloody hell are you doing, girl? What's happening to you? You selfish, little bitch."

Then I remember he slammed the phone down. I burst into tears as the realisation hit me. I had nobody.

The next day, I joined Médecins Sans Frontières. I packed away my life, physically and metaphorically, and left the country. I didn't know for how long, possibly forever, or until I did what was necessary to get her back.

I had spent the past five years in some of the world's most dangerous conflicts, in regions where the poor never had a voice and always paid the price for the bigoted minds of men. Nothing shocked me anymore. Nothing. My emotional rock bottom was losing her. It became my reference point for absolute misery, wherever I was.

In those years, I became a woman, forged from the energy of a girl, but my own possibilities were dulled by her loss. Yet, I kept going, on and on. "Keep going, Kirstie," I would tell myself in the dark of the night. Just keep going.

But Rwanda was different. If I were to describe any place on earth that felt evil, it would be Rwanda. The country had been amid a bloody civil war for the past five years, and even the squalor and hopelessness of Somalia hadn't prepared me for its own vile twist of logic and revenge.

The majority Hutu tribe was systematically eliminating the Tutsi minority. It was an extermination supported from the highest echelons of government to the lowest levels of society. In recent weeks, the country had fallen into chaos. Hutus would massacre their Tutsi neighbours, murdering people who had been friends only months before. And if they didn't kill them, they were killed themselves. A blood-red mist had descended upon the nation, a collective loss of consciousness and responsibility where nobody and everybody was to blame. It was a nightmare where the ends justified the means, and machetes were the weapon of choice because bullets were expensive.

The Tutsis were treated as insects, and every government radio station proclaimed, through crackling radio sets across the country, the great deed you would do if you butchered that small Tutsi child as she slept next door. They urged people to keep slicing and hacking until they were all gone.

But this war was different in another way, and it would set the standard for the depravities to come. The warmongers had discovered another weapon, a weapon that was free, unlimited, and impossible to fight against: rape.

Violation of women became a means to degrade and humiliate the motherhood of a nation. Rape became the norm rather than the exception, and Uwimana was just another victim of the Hutu army as they dehumanized the Tutsi women on their way to eliminating an entire nation. Most girls were murdered after they were abused or fucked to death. The fortunate ones survived, though most became HIV-positive. Those who became pregnant had their babies aborted through beatings and the vile intrusions of rifle barrels.

Because of this I never went anywhere without Gus. He was a former paratrooper, a nurse, and my guardian.

Yes, Uwimana was one of the lucky ones. She had survived.

**

"Waa...! Waaahh...!"

I thought it was a fragment of a dream, a disturbed cry from the depths of my mind. But it wasn't.

Gus awakened me with a jolt, almost throwing me to the floor.

"Come now! She's bloody miscarrying!"

I shielded my eyes, blinded by the beam of his torch. Then he was gone.

When I arrived, Muteteli was holding her hand. I saw her digging her fingernails into the old lady's arm, drawing blood. The old lady just allowed, as if taking on the pain would lessen it for the child. They screamed at each other in their language.

Then the hollow, weak girl became even emptier as she expelled her baby in one big, bloody, excruciating push.

"Waaaaahh!"

The foetus fell onto the concrete floor with a splat. It was dark and grey. Or rather, she was dark and grey. She was a girl. Almost instantly, she expelled the placenta as the dying matter left her body. The bed became a sponge of red. The colour spread as the mattress absorbed the remaining speck of hope and life from her.

Instantly, she understood what had happened. She closed her eye and scrunched up her face, pushing all the tears and pain into the pit of her stomach. All we could hear was her panting breath and Muteteli quietly reciting a prayer to herself.

I needed to act quickly, but I had nothing. Everything was gone. I struggled to think of what to do.

Then, in the void between hope and despair, chaos erupted.

"Fucking shit, they're coming!"

Gus peeked out of the blinds, breaking the near silence.

"What?"

"Troops. Army troops. We've got to get the fuck out of here!"

He looked at me, waiting for me to take the lead. My heart sank as another blow hit. In that moment, I was torn between what had just happened and the reality of being discovered.

I froze.

"Kirstie, we've got to get out,"

I stood there, as if rooted to the floor.

Then suddenly, I broke through my paralysis. God knows how.

"Get her in the Land-Rover. We've got to get her out of here. Drop everything. Let's go. Now!"

Gus looked at me incredulously.

"Christ, K! She's fucking going to bleed to death. Fucking look at her?"

I didn't need to. I knew she was haemorrhaging before my very eyes. It wasn't supposed to be like this.

"Look, she's dead anyway if we don't go!" I screamed. "But

I'm not putting in our report we left her behind to fucking bleed to death!"

"I'll dress her. Go get the kit we can carry. Start the Land-Rover. We'll leave in ten minutes."

I shouted my orders with a courage that appeared out of nowhere.

The next ten minutes felt like an eternity as I struggled to apply some used dressings and stem the flow of blood. The poor child mumbled to herself, and miraculously, the bleeding began to subside. My hand trembled like an autumn leaf in the breeze, coated in her blood. In my haste, I hadn't bothered to put on gloves.

"Come on, K. Job to do. Job to do," I whispered to myself, attempting to calm down.

Uwimama looked at me, confused and empty.

I unhooked her saline drip and placed it on the child's lap. Cradling her in my arms, I stumbled down the stairwell and dumped her into the back of the Land-Rover. She was as light as a paper bag. Gus kicked everything out of the vehicle onto the ground and beckoned the old woman to get in. Muteteli was unsure of what to do. The woman looked scared and confused. She knew they were coming. She hesitated at the rear of the vehicle.

I screamed at her, "Fucking get in! If they find you, you'll be dead too."

She didn't move, the horror of running away too unbearable for her to contemplate.

"Look, I need you to translate if we get stopped. Please get in. Please?"

Finally, she relented.

Five minutes later, we were speeding through the night on potholed, bomb-blasted tracks toward the Zaire border. With every turn and dip in the road, Uwimana winced and cried.

I had done it. I had done what that woman had asked. But was it worth it?

Of course, it was. She was my daughter, and I was determined to get her back.

Chapter 8

Marky came back home drunk one night and I smelt it on him. It was a rose petal of a scent, a fragrance with an aftermath of sandalwood. After he whipped his shirt off and threw it into the laundry basket, it was gone.

I lay beside him for the next two hours thinking about it. I was too scared to pull his shirt back out of the basket to smell it, in case he woke up. I pushed the worry to the back of my mind, wrapped my hands around my tummy and tried to sleep.

But I couldn't.

In the morning when he had left, I retrieved it from under the sweaty socks and knickers, but the fragrance had evaporated. I felt so guilty doubting him. Later that night I tried to comfort him, but he didn't want any of it. We argued again, over something and nothing. I told him to go fuck himself because he wouldn't tell me what was going on, go fuck himself up his tight backside. Then I stormed off.

So, Miss Bump and me slept alone together, again. Oh, and she was a Miss. I believed that mad woman on the farm completely. Marky sulked on the mattress on the living room floor.

At first I took no notice. I asked him where he had been. He just gave me a load of bullocks about leaving work and going on the piss with his mates. I don't know whether he was just enjoying his last days of freedom, before we finally became a family, or there was something else.

A week later it happened again. He came in stinking of the same smell. This time he became aggressive and told me to mind my own effing business, and stood staggering around in the kitchen and slurring his words. Maybe it was because I was at home all day, incubating the baby and cramming in some last revision. He resented it, didn't see it as proper work. I was close to qualifying. His research was going badly, problems with grants, students, everything by all accounts. We hadn't had sex for months. Bizarrely it wasn't me that had lost the appetite, far from it. He just didn't take any interest anymore.

One night I couldn't take it. He lay next to me, in a huff over something, staring at the ceiling for the umpteenth night running. He didn't want to play.

"What's the matter ? You used to like it."

Silence.

"Is it the baby ? Are you worried you'll hurt the baby ? Well, you won't. I know. My cervix is completely closed. She is completely safe."

"Or he is safe." he answered sarcastically.

"Look, what's the matter. Is it us ?"

After a pause he replied,

"No."

That night I hardly slept. My minded conjured up horrible scenarios and what the true meaning of 'no' meant.

**

I thought she would respond with something like, "Oh, stop being so silly," or "It's just your hormones, pregnancy can make you feel this way, Pet." But she didn't.

On the phone, there was a gasp from my Mum, followed by an eternal pause before she finally spoke.

She didn't say anything I expected.

"Kirstie, the choices you make now will shape the rest of your life. I'd rather have a daughter who's a good mother, even if she's a single one, than a daughter who's unhappy and living a lie."

Her words were direct and unwavering.

I didn't know how to respond. Her certainty and frankness left me speechless.

"Don't cling to false hope just for our sake. Resolve things quickly, one way or another," she added.

As if discussing the weather, she continued, "I once discovered your father was involved with Tracy Henshaw. It happened a few years after we got married." She emphasized the word 'involved', employing its broadest, biblical interpretation.

I was gob-smacked.

"Dad! What! Mrs. Henshaw? The woman in the newsagents?"

She didn't say anything, but her silence spoke volumes.

"I put an end to that right away,"

My mother spat out the words.

"She was a little tart, she was,"

Wow, I didn't know what to say. The idea of Dad having an affair seemed the most ludicrous thing possible. He was, well, Dad – dull, predictable, and utterly lovely.

"Listen, dear, there are many Tracy Henshaws in this world. Don't let them trample over good people like you and me. They're just... little sluts."

Dad and Tracy Henshaw! It was shocking, but not as shocking as Mum swearing. I'd never heard her utter any profanity before.

I spent the rest of the evening contemplating her words, sipping on green tea, an unexpected craving, and waddling around the house as if wearing a fat suit.

Marky was gone again, and I struggled to make sense of it all.

Deep down, though, I knew my mother was right about what I needed to do.

**

Outside, rain battered against the window, forming rivulets that cascaded down the glass. I lay prostrate on the sofa, observing the water's chase, feeling utterly defeated.

It was a November Friday night, and once again, I found myself alone in the house. Marky was out drinking, as usual. I knew exactly where he was, thanks to my little snitch.

Summoning the energy, I sat up. I was only two months away from the big day, and the kicks in my ribs were becoming unbearable. I stood up, determined. Tonight was the night, that little shit.

Grabbing his car keys, I set out to sort it out– one way or another.

Upon arriving at the pub, I was accosted at the entrance by a group of drunk students, shaking loose change-filled tins in front of me. The rain continued to pour down.

"Children in Need! Children in Need!"

"I'm sure they are, but they can remain in bloody need!" I replied, unamused by their antics.

"Ohh... somebody's a party pooper!" taunted a heavily intoxicated girl, unsteady on her feet. My mother would have described her as "all unfastened top and cleavage."

I shot her a piercing glare; I wasn't in the mood.

Standing at the entrance, I hesitated to enter, my hair dripping from the rain. Taking a deep breath, I pushed my way through.

As soon as he saw me, Marky's face registered a mix of shock, surprise, and then feigned excitement. He leaped up from the table and stumbled towards me.

"You didn't mention you were coming down?" he said clearly flustered.

I paused before I answered.

"I just needed to get out of the house for the bit. Get a bit of fresh air, see the outside world for once."

"Ohh."

", and get into the fundraising spirit" I lied.

He stood there, not knowing what to do. His gang of mates sat gawping, and looking embarrassed. All conversation had stopped the moment I waddled into the bar

"So, aren't you going to introduce me?" I gestured toward his drinking buddies.

"Oh, yeah, of course," he replied and scratched the back of his head, like Dad did when feeling uncomfortable or hiding something from my mother. And Marky was definitely hiding something.

"Well, this is Tony, working on the same project as me. You've met him before, I believe," Marky introduced.

"Hi, Tony,"

I greeted him with as much cheerfulness as I could muster. Tony offered a wave, as if polishing an invisible window. I could only describe him as having a pale complexion, an effeminate demeanour (though not gay), and an obsession with television and pop music. Despite being in his thirties, he seemed stuck in his teenage years, walking with a distinct flamboyance that accentuated his height. Tony wore shabby trainers, a stretched-out polo shirt, and ill-fitting jeans. He looked as if he was wearing someone else's clothes. He was also my blabbermouth.

"You look like you're ready to pop! How much longer now?" he asked, with lips too thin for my liking.

I glanced down at my protruding belly.

"Oh, about two more months," I replied, and from their expressions, I could sense they anticipated my waters breaking right then and there in the pub.

"Yes, we're both eagerly awaiting the arrival of our new child," I said, attempting to suppress the sarcasm, but it seeped out.

Marky shuffled on his feet and continued the introductions.

"And this is John, and this is John. The two Johns!"

Marky had spoken of them before, but this was my first-time meeting both. John Williams was small with tightly curled hair, resembling a schoolboy fresh out of class. He drank excessively and seemed to have an opinion on everything. John Dunlop, on the other hand, was the complete opposite. With a clean-cut appearance that belonged in the 1950s, he seldom spoke and from what I had heard, had no opinion on anything. Fashion-wise, the two Johns were at opposite ends of the John spectrum. The former wore black jeans and a faded biker's jacket that showed signs of a motorcycle accident. The latter sported an acrylic jumper, reminiscent of an outdated Christmas gift, even by late '80s standards.

I waved hello.

John W. greeted me with a broad smile, while John D. averted my gaze. He was seemingly shy or perhaps just rude.

Then Marky introduced her.. the sole girl in the group.

"...and this is Corrine. She's studying for a PhD in my team.

107

She's from Ireland."

She was in her mid-twenties, possessed a slender frame and a stylish cropped ginger bob. Her fair skin was devoid of makeup. She wore dungarees and polished Dr. Martens shoes. When she leaned over to shake my hand, her breasts almost spilled out of her top – braless, held in place only by a white cropped t-shirt. Strangely, she exuded a certain sense of style.

Then I smelt it on her; the adulterous stink. She reeked of it. Maybe because I was hypersensitive to the scent. No, she wasn't stylish, she was a complete and utter, fucking slag and at that very moment I knew it was her. She was a dirty fucking bitch and I hated her there and then.

"So, you're Marky's student then ?"

She pushed a strand of hair behind her ear in a nervous way.

"Yes, sort of. "

When she deflected my gaze, I was certain of it.

I'd thought I'd feel angry, hurt. But I didn't. I just felt trapped and cornered as they grinned at me with insincere, fake smiles, as if it was all my fault. It wasn't all my fault.

Suddenly the music in the bar melted into a hum and I could feel the life drain from me, leaving me with an emptiness inside.

"Are you okay ?" she asked.

I stared at her blankly, conscious my mouth was half open, as I struggled to reply.

"Sorry... sorry I've got to use the ladies room."

I almost ran to the toilet.

Inside I locked the cubicle and burst into tears.

So, there she was, the girl who had stolen my Marky. The little bitch. I wanted to storm back out, throw Marty's beer over her and shout at the top of my voice, what a slut she was and make a big, embarrassing scene. Then, he'd feel as I did: humiliated and worthless. But I didn't. It wouldn't have made a jot of difference. I rubbed Bump and cried onto her, my tears falling like raindrops onto my descended belly. I sat on the toilet seat for I don't know how long, I can't remember. It all became a bit of a blur.

Suddenly, she knocked on the cubicle door with soft, gentle taps.

"Kirstie, are you okay in there? We're getting worried."

I unfastened the door and stepped out.

"Oh, my love. You've been crying. What's wrong?"

Her words surprised me, spoken with tenderness in a soft Irish lilt that soothed like a nurse's voice.

I remembered my mother's advice.

"So, you're the bitch who's been fucking my husband, then?"

She recoiled as if struck, unable to find words. Her silence spoke volumes, confirming what I already knew.

"I... I don't know what to say," she mumbled.

"Sorry would be a good start," I spluttered between sobs.

But she didn't say it because she wasn't sorry at all. I had been in her position before. She had fallen for Marky's toxic charm and was completely ensnared. As the magnitude of the situation dawned on her, her eyes welled up. An innocent affair with her boss had now escalated into the dissolution of a marriage. She had blood on her hands, and she knew it.

Tears trickled down her cheeks as she wiped them away with the back of her hand.

In that moment, I couldn't help but feel sorry for her. She was just another victim.

"I... I... I'll split up with him," she sniffed and looked up at me, her eyes suddenly red, as if hoping it would make everything better.

"Too late. Far too late," I replied, surprised at the coldness in my tone.

"He's made his bed, and he's going to have to lie in it. With you."

"He's damaged goods now," I continued, almost laughing with a surprising sense of relief.

Then, without understanding why, I did something. It felt natural and necessary in that bleak moment we shared together. I hugged her. Yes, I hugged her.

"Be careful. If he deceived me, he'll deceive you," I whispered into her ear.

She nodded ever so faintly.

Together, we left the toilets. As I walked out of the pub, I glanced back to see the look of abject horror on my husband's face as his web of deception unravelled before him, in front of his friends.

A drunk student shook a collection bucket in his face. All I could see was him shaking his head, filled with despair.

Two hours later, he stumbled back home, completely intoxicated. We argued into the early hours. He pleaded, cried, and tried to convince me. But I wasn't having any of it.

The next day, he left, and from that point on, our communication was limited to cold exchanges via the legal profession.

Now, it was just me and Bump. So, Bump and I moved on.

**

"Congratulations, Doctor McBride. I'm so damn proud of you, Petal!" My mother held me by my shoulders and gave me a loving shake.

"Doctor Bowen-Wright," I replied. "I'm going to keep his name."

She scowled at me.

"I always wanted a double-barrelled name," I joked. "And anyway, it's the only thing he's given me, apart from this." I pointed at Bump.

She didn't seem pleased. Dad turned away, sensing a potential scene. But Mum didn't want to spoil my big day and responded in her menacing tone, "We'll talk about it later, Pet."

I was now a Doctor, with a capital D, a fully-fledged medic. Standing in Southampton Guildhall after the graduation ceremony, I could see the immense pride in my parents' eyes. Dad beamed, dressed in his new Burton's suit. Mum looked stunning in her cream-coloured dress and the new hat she had gone all the way to Sheffield to get fitted, "from a proper milliner, no less."

But I wasn't alone. I had an escort, in a way.

"This is Dave,"

I introduced a very polished Mr. Hudson.

"Top one," Dave signalled to my father, who didn't know how to respond but was overjoyed, nonetheless.

"Top one as well." he replied back and went off to find some food.

"Shall I get some drinks in?" Dave announced and swaggered off to the champagne bar to get a complimentary round.

"Is he your new...?" my mother asked as soon as they were out of earshot.

"No, he's not. He certainly isn't. He's just Dave."

Mum frowned at me.

"Look, Dave was the first person I met when I arrived five years ago, and he helped me then. We've stayed in touch ever since. He's my chaperone today, and it's all proper and above board."

Before we could continue Dave and Dad returned with drinks and snacks.

I could see Mum was bursting to ask. After Dave placed the tray on the cocktail table, amazingly without any disaster; she pounced.

"So Dave," she said, saying his name as it was a foreign word. "What do you do ?"

Suddenly, Dave was transfixed for anything to say. I could see his face freezing as he struggled to find the appropriate words.

I stared at him.

He gawped back, open mouthed like a fish.

"Stuff," he finally said.

"Stuff?"

"Dave is an entrepreneur," I intervened to help him out.

"Yes," he replied, "I mostly entrepreneur."

"But currently, I'm fitting tyres at KwikFit,"

Mum didn't even bother replying and turned to me. Dave dived into his champagne and hors d'oeuvres. He wasn't remotely bothered. Free food and drink were enough to keep him happy.

"So, what's next for my young Doctor? Only six weeks to go,"

I knew the question was coming, but truthfully, I didn't have the answer myself.

"I have some work in the A&E department at the hospital, just for a few weeks. I want to get started before the baby arrives."

Her pursed expression showed her disapproval. In fact, she seemed disgusted, as if she had smelled something unpleasant.

"Mum, it's going to be alright. Once I start, I can take maternity leave. But I need to begin the position, and it's a good opportunity."

"Well, you should be taking it easier now."

"I will, Mum. I have the rest of my life to take it easy."

"You wish!" she scoffed. "You don't know what's going to hit you."

And that was the end of it.

Mum always made a big deal out of some things. Looking back, maybe I should have listened to her, just this once.

Chapter 9

"Slow down!"

The vehicle veered off the broken track and crashed through the dense scrub-land. Branches rattled under the body of the Land-Rover as it crashed through the darkness.

Gus didn't reply. He was too busy squinting into the dimness in front of him, a blackness lit by nothing other than a slowly waning moon, which turned the landscape to a monochrome tapestry. The car jolted back and forth over the rocks, rolling up and down like a ship in a heavy sea. With each jolt I thought my back would break.

"Why don't we stick to the road?" I screamed.

By 'road' I meant the loosely defined pathway through the bush, nothing more than a broken rut.

"Look, you have to slow the fuck down! She's bleeding like crazy back there!"

He paid no attention.

I could hear her wincing and shrieking with each bump the Land-Rover crushed over.

In frustration, I flicked on the cabin light.

"Are you trying to get us all bloody killed?" Gus exploded.

I swiftly turned the light off, plunging the cabin back into darkness.

Gus squinted into the blackness.

"There were lights back there," he mumbled to himself, momentarily slowing down until his night vision returned.

"Sorry," he continued, turning to me. "I need to get into the zone. It's been a while since I've done something like this."

I didn't understand what he meant, so I let him focus. He drove the vehicle across the scrub-land, aiming for the border as if he were crash-landing a plane. After what felt like an eternity, but was probably only ten minutes, the battered Land-Rover finally re-joined the main road, offering relative calm. Though, the road still resembled a farmer's potholed track.

I could hear the old lady being sick in the back, but we had to keep going.

"Why are you going so bloody fast?"

He sighed, clearly frustrated.

"Because we have to cross the border before dawn."

"Okay, okay," I muttered.

We sat in silence for two hours. The old woman fell asleep, and Uwimana remained awake but quiet, embracing Muteteli while mumbling about her loss. Her clothes were as stained as a used tampon.

In a moment of comparative calm, I asked him, partially to hear his voice.

"Why did you leave the Army?"

Gus didn't immediately reply, but eventually, he answered.

"I decided it was better to help people live than help them die."

I waited for a moment before continuing.

"What about peacekeeping?"

"Nobody ever brought peace to the world with a gun in their hand. Look at bloody America," he replied, smiling.

Then he turned the tables on me.

"Why did you run away?"

I didn't respond.

"Because you're running, aren't you? Just like me? You've always been running, haven't you?"

I ignored him and squinted into the darkness. Gus had asked me the same question before, and I had ignored him then. Truthfully, I wasn't running away from anything; I was moving toward her. Each step was a step closer. It was the only thing that kept me going.

In the distance, the sun began to rise, casting a faint smudge of warmth and hope on the horizon. Gus continued talking to me, mostly to keep himself awake, but I wasn't listening. As his words became a jumble, I slowly drifted off, my chin dropping onto my chest, and no matter how hard I tried to fight it, I went to sleep.

**

The jolt nearly took my head off.

The vehicle screeched to a halt on the gravel road. People screamed in Kinyarwanda, and the windshield shattered into a lattice of crystals. Then my window collapsed inward with the crash of a rifle-butt.

Still in a dream state I stumbled out of the car, and was dragged across the gritty stones by a screaming man, ripping my knees as he pulled me along. I looked up. He had a machete in his hand.

He screamed at me again, but I couldn't comprehend and he shouted more.

Then, I understood.

Another man yanked Uwimana out of the car, as if she were a piece of meat. The old lady protested with screams. With a sickening crunch, he shattered Muteteli's face using the butt of his rifle. She crumpled to the ground, clutching her bloody, broken face. I couldn't believe what was happening.

The air filled with screams—mine, the old lady's, and the two thugs spewing vitriolic threats in a strange tongue.

"Stop! Stop!" I bellowed. "We are medics! We want to help!"

"We want to help!"

They paid no attention.

They didn't understand. They wouldn't understand. I rushed over and pulled the girl away from the man. His eyes burned with hatred. Sweat covered his face.

Then, I saw Gus being dragged from the driver's seat. He had a look of fear in his eyes. He stared down the barrel of the trembling rifle. The assailant looked no older than a boy and not much older than the girl. He locked eyes on the boy struggling to keep the weapon steady. Gus understood in an instant; youth could be unpredictable, ready to perform a big act and step into the bloodied shoes of manhood.

The boy could barely hold the rifle steady.

"Leave the girl alone. She means nothing to you. Leave her

be!" Gus pleaded.

He ignored Gus's calm and measured plea, waving the rifle menacingly. He acted like a man, but in his eyes I could see the fear of a boy.

"Inyenzi. Inyenzi," they chanted in unison, waving at the girl. I later realised it meant 'cockroach.'

His older brother stared at him with a frown of displeasure.

Then the boy snapped.

Gus collided with the side of the Land-Rover, struck by the rifle's blow to his kidneys. The older boy seized his hand, extended Gus's arm, and raised his machete, glinting silver in the rising sun. He paused, poised to bring it down with one swift chop.

The Hutu boy locked eyes with me.

In that fleeting moment, everything balanced on a tipping point in time.

Beside Uwimana, the old lady stood screaming.

Gus closed his eyes, bracing for the blade to strike. It all merged into one ugly mellee.

Then, I let her go.

I released my hand from hers and raised it in the air.

In that split second, I betrayed her.

Suddenly, it was quiet.

All I could hear was my own breath.

They exchanged words and pointed into the distance.

Slowly, they led Uwimana away.

The girl walked away with a heart-breaking dignity. They took the old lady as well, although she held even less value to them. Both were worth next to nothing.

All I could do was hug Gus.

He mouthed a hollow "thank you" to me.

We drove back in silence. Tears streamed down my face as the engine hummed, and the Land-Rover rolled toward the border.

He gently placed his hand on my knee and gave it a reassuring stroke. I remember pushing it away.

We both knew they were dead, their lives gone; but not before they had been degraded, and made to feel worthless. Their souls had become more drops of blood swimming in an ocean of death and retribution in a crumbling nation.

The shame would follow me for the rest of my life, but it wouldn't be the worst thing I would do to get her back.

At that moment, the act cancelled out in my mind what I had done, the intervention I had made. It was a twisted logic that propelled me forward, always forward. As the scorching sun rose above the border, it sank in my heart, which I was sure was growing darker with each passing day.

**

I listened and absorbed it all, taking the criticism from my mother.

"Look, you're taking on too much. You only have four weeks to go,"

It had been a terrible day at the hospital, but finally it was my last day. It had been complete bedlam. There had been a home match and Casualty was swamped with drunk, leering football fans cluttering up A&E with the aftermath of street fights with their rivals. I even had to get Security to separate them in the waiting area and prevent them all kicking off again, which was pretty pathetic.

Living just a few miles from The Dell, I knew better than to venture out during a home match, especially a local derby with Portsmouth. But foolishly, I went to work, feeling invincible in my heavily pregnant state. Strangely, being pregnant gave me an air of invulnerability. I was treated delicately, most of the time, and even some of the drunks became kinder once they realised I was about to give birth. One intoxicated fan, beer can in hand, even offered me his seat, which was rather sweet, despite the large shard of glass sticking out of his forehead.

"No thanks, mate. I have a job to do. You seem like you need a good sit-down more than I do. I'll attend to you in a moment," I replied, noticing his injury.

During the first half of my shift, it was a relief to be away from the chaos on the streets, but things only worsened. As the pubs began emptying, the situation grew more absurd. I could pinpoint the exact moment when *The Churchill* pub, across from the stadium, expelled its drinkers, as a wave of drunk, time-wasting individuals flooded our hospital. Thankfully, when the alcoholic tsunami hit, I had only two hours left to go.

Not all the drunks were pleasant. Some stumbled in, smiling one moment, and snarling the next. One particularly irate drunk was sick in front of me, drenching me in beer and the remnants of his stomach contents.

And to top it all off, there was a flu outbreak. People came in with raging fevers, complaining because they couldn't see a GP on a Saturday.

"Mum, some of these people should just pull themselves together," I remarked.

One couple was so furious that I had to refer them to the consultant to resolve the matter. I had never encountered such an angry woman before.

"Look, Mum, I have time to rest now. I'm finished,"

Then she fell silent. I sensed she was about to ask something, in her nosy, protective way.

"Where is he now?" she finally inquired.

"Gone," I replied.

She would never ask about Marky again. It was final.

"I'll be down soon," she said.

"What about Dad?"

"He'll just have to learn to make beans on toast himself."

"But Dad is useless around the house."

"Needs must, Petal. Needs must," she replied, and the conversation ended abruptly as she hung up.

At least I had Mum. She was still there for me. For a moment, the house didn't feel as empty. The ticking of the clock was no longer as ominous. I rubbed my tummy and chatted to her until I fell asleep on the sofa, too exhausted to move.

When I woke up, it began. Bump was coming.

**

Gus hadn't changed much in the twenty-odd years since we were in Rwanda. His ginger hair was now mostly grey, with a hint of pink, like a white shirt mistakenly washed with colours. His complexion was more weathered than I remembered, but he still had that sparkle in his eyes, and his South African accent had only slightly softened.

"You look fantastic," he complimented me.

The wine bar was filling up, mostly with businessmen and couples engaged in secret office romances, from what I could see.

"Don't bullshit me, Gus. You're such a cheeky bugger,"

He appeared offended by my response.

"No, really, you look great," he insisted. And for once, I allowed myself to accept the compliment, even though I knew it wasn't entirely true. Youth had long abandoned me. Now, it was a desperate battle against age, armed only with moisturisers and creams.

"How have you been keeping?" I asked, knowing it a coded question.

Gus took it at face value.

"Still trying to train the perfect nurse. Still plodding on. Still trying to piece together the broken," he replied.

"And you?"

I hesitated, unsure of where to begin. So, I started with something I knew he could handle.

"I'm actually doing quite well. Long story short, I have a GP practice in Poole with thirty thousand patients, a nice house, and cats."

"Wow, your mother must be proud?"

"She was. She passed away a few years ago, and Dad is in a care home. I don't think he understands much now."

"I'm sorry. I know you were close," Gus sympathised.

"Thanks," I replied. Even now, talking about it hurt, and Gus could tell.

"Married?"

He asked, as if it were the last thing on his mind.

"Once a long time ago. All in the past now," I answered, side-stepping the issue.

Gus sat up, as if prodded.

When we left the conflict zone, we grew even closer. But then, for various reasons, we drifted apart. We were never a real couple, or so I thought. Each time he opened his heart to me, I accepted it and then pushed him away. Eventually, we went in separate directions. One final night, fuelled by a cheap bottle of vodka beneath the Cape Town sunset, he tearfully confessed that he was completely and utterly in love with me.

I wasn't shocked, but at the time, I coldly rejected his advances. It was more than I could bear, burdening someone else with my problems. I crushed his heart and trampled the petals of his hope with my obsession to find her. It was just another terrible thing I had done over the years, one of many. Yet, there was still a connection between us that, in a strange way, brought us back together. Over the years, we maintained contact through emails, letters, the occasional drunken phone call, but this was the first time we had met face-to-face in over two decades.

I was nervous to see him again. No, that's not accurate. I was terrified. I spent the entire morning getting my hair styled properly, adding highlights with a chemical russet colour. Dressed in the best outfit *Pur Una* had to offer, I didn't look too bad, or so I thought. But what did I know? It had been so long. I felt strange, as if I were on a first date all over again.

Initially, I thought he had stood me up. As the minutes ticked by, waiting alone in the wine bar, my anxiety grew. To make matters worse, a man sitting at the bar kept glancing at me furtively between sips of his coffee, typing away on his laptop. I tried to occupy myself rearranging the contents of my handbag, which was, as usual, a mess, and sipping my red wine.

Just as I was about to give up and leave, Gus had walked in. And boy, did he look stunning.

As the hour passed, we engaged in conversation, skirting around the main topic. But Gus already knew what I wanted to discuss.

"Look, you didn't bring me here for idle chitchat and catching up. What's up, K?" he finally asked.

I took a deep breath and gulped down some Shiraz, mustering my courage.

"Gus, I need to tell you something. I need to confide in someone."

Gus, with his nursing instincts kicking in, leant forward as if every word I said mattered.

I told him everything, or at least everything I could without putting us both in danger.

Then cutting to the chase he asked.

"Was it one of the reasons you pushed me way ?"

I owed enough to Gus to give him an honest answer.

"Yes." I replied, suddenly unable to look him in the eye.

I could sense the relief in his body language. Suddenly he relaxed and collapsed into his chair.

"Kirstie, you silly, bloody, lovely girl. Why didn't you say ? It's no big deal."

He said 'girl' as if he really meant it. I hadn't been called a girl in years.

I didn't answer, but just picked my nails and stared past him into the street outside.

"Are you sure she's your daughter ?" he continued.

"Yes, absolutely."

"How?"

"Look, Gus. I just know. I can't say why."

He sat there contemplating all I had said, letting it sink in. I could see him probing it in his mind for weaknesses.

As always he came straight to the point.

"Why did you give her away?"

"I had to," was my simple reply.

He didn't ask the question again, but I knew he was thinking it.

"Does she know?" he asked. It was the same question that had plagued me. Did she know? Was Mutti just playing with me, using it as another twist in her game? I still didn't have an answer.

"One of the adoption agreements was that I would never reveal myself as her birth mother, unless she sought me out and asked," I explained, offering the best response I could.

"What are you going to do?" Gus asked, his concern palpable.

"I'll do what I've been doing all along—wait and hope," I replied.

He reached across the table and held my hand, just like he used to.

"If you need any help, just call me. You know that, right? Whatever you need, even if it's just someone to listen," he offered sincerely.

"Of course," I replied.

And with a parting kiss, I confused Gus further and fanned the embers of his affection for me. But this time, I didn't care.

**

"Look, I'm fully bloody dilated!" I screamed, my voice piercing through the room as I gripped the mattress tightly, almost tearing off my nails.

The medic looked at me nonchalantly.

"You can't be ready yet. We've only just induced you. Why don't you take a warm bath? It'll help speed things up," the young doctor with the spotty face responded, his tone both patronising and provoking.

"Why don't you just go fuck yourself!" I bellowed back, recognizing him as a fellow Southampton graduate from a few years ahead of me in med school. Not the ideal situation to encounter a fellow alumnus.

He took a step back, as if anticipating an explosion.

"Young man, I believe my daughter knows her own body," my mother interjected, using that condescending and undermining tone she could master so well.

"And may I remind you, she is a doctor herself," she added, delivering the final put-down.

The message was received loud and clear, and he began to retreat from the presence of two furious Yorkshire women.

Suddenly, my screams intensified to the point where foam started to trickle from my mouth, and Mum said my face turned a fiery shade of red. The next thing I recall is the midwife entering the room with another student, who observed my efforts as part of his "on the job experience." She watched in awe as I pushed with a scream so powerful it felt like I was being torn in half.

In between contractions, I lay there gasping for air, feeling like a woman nearing the finish line of a marathon she had never trained for. And then, suddenly, before I thought it would never end—she was out.

The room reverberated with the cries of a new-born baby. My daughter had arrived, expressing her discontent and indignation of it all.

"There, Pet, I told you gas and air was all you needed. It's like shelling peas, it is. The next one will be even easier," Mum reassured me, her words causing me to stare at her in disbelief.

"There won't be another bloody one!" I declared, and then I simply laughed. I laughed and laughed as a wave of relief washed over me.

Mum kissed my sweaty forehead as the midwife placed my daughter in my arms.

That eccentric farm-woman had been right all along. It was a girl. Tears streamed down my face as I chuckled. Her complexion was as red as a ripe Cox's apple, and she had a shock of ginger hair. She was simply breath-taking. It was just the two of us now—no more Mrs. Bump. Rebecca was born.

She latched on and suckled for the first time, and it all felt so natural. My focus shifted entirely to her, and even as the nurse stitched me back together, I felt nothing, but the presence of her.

Mum sat contently in an old, worn-out chair in the birthing room, grinning to herself, appearing to be the proudest grandmother whoever lived.

Chapter 10

"So, how was your first month in General Practice? Was it as you expected?" she asked, prompting me for a response.

I pondered my answer for a moment. It had certainly been different, unlike the order and calm I was accustomed to in Heidelberg.

"Well, it's different from Germany," I replied. "It's more..."

"...like bloody bedlam?" she said finishing my sentence, with a sigh.

"I'm sorry. I should have prepared you better for how things are over here,"

I laughed.

"Yes, it's more fluid here," I said tactfully.

I suppose it was kind of her to invite me into her home. Initially, I had been unsure about accepting the invitation, fearing it might be a trick. But I noticed how different she was from her work persona. Here, she seemed relaxed, even calm. She got up from the table and went over to stir whatever was cooking on the stove. To be honest, it didn't smell very appetising.

"The trouble here in the UK is that we're being pulled from pillar to post with this bloody government," she commented.

"Pillar to post?" I inquired.

"Sorry, it's an expression. It means being pulled in many directions," she explained.

"If only Labour had done a proper job, we wouldn't have this shambles of a bloody government," she vented, taking a big gulp from her glass.

"And what with damn Brexit and all that." she added.

"Your country has maybe been a bit silly," I replied.

She took another sip of her drink and returned to stirring the meal, suddenly becoming quiet.

"Yes we all do stupid things at times, things we regret." she said cryptically.

There was something I couldn't quite place in her features,

something she was hiding behind a curtain, but I didn't know what. But it was kind of her to invite me over. I didn't expect her to be kind. Mutti didn't say she could be kind.

"You've a lovely house."

"Thank you."

Then she went back to cutting something up and was quiet suddenly.

Her house was well, not unclean. But it was untidy, in a Bohemian, messy kind a way. Celtic, I think she called it. Back home she would have been a Green, I was sure, a very dark green, a housewife hippy green.

"Your house isn't how I imagined."

She paused, and then answered.

"I have a separate my work from my personal life. I have to keep them apart, for my own sanity."

Looking back I don't know why she said it. She didn't need to justify anything.

Nobody does.

We sat down at a large, very old, oak-table. It looked as ancient as the cottage. It looked completely in keeping with kitchen, which had a rustic and lived in feel. The kitchen walls were covered with watercolours and chalk sketches - all arranged in a ' thrown-on-the-wall ' sort of way. All were in the same style; a gentle, wafting wave of flowing colour.

"Whose are these ? " I asked.

She looked embarrassed and pulled the hair back over her head and rose from the table to stir the pot again, which was now erupting over the stove.

"They're mine." she replied.

"I could have gone to Art College, or maybe should have."

"That would have been so different," I said, stating the obvious.

"Yes, but I chose Medicine. And we all have to live with the choices we make, don't we ?" she said with a sigh.

"And keep our promises," she added softly, almost to herself.

"What did you do after you graduated ?" I asked.

126

I knew the answer, Mutti had told me, but I wanted to hear from her, to see whether she would put a gloss on it. I wanted to hear it from her own lips.

"Well, " she replied, "I joined Medicine San Frontier, and toured Africa mostly with the charity, and did other aid work.

"Oh."

"You seemed surprised ?"

"Sorry, I didn't know you did that."

"As you can see from all this... " she replied, waving her hand at all the hippy artefacts in the kitchen," I'm a bit of an idealist. There are still some of us left in the world."

Then she told me of the horrors of the 90s, told me stories that shocked and disturbed me. I'm surprised to say stories that left me in awe. But they were all lies. It wasn't what Mutti had told me. It was just more lies and falsehoods.

"So after ten years of travelling, I came back home. I trained for General Practice, and the rest is well, history."

I didn't know what to say. So I sat there and said nothing.

"I just became sick with living out of a holdall for more than a decade. '

"Holdall ?"

"A rucksack ? It's called a holdall, but when you try and live your life out of it you realise it holds fuck-all, excuse my language."

I laughed. It was the first time I'd heard her swear. I didn't imagine she swore, but here she was ' fucking and bloodying ' like a soldier. Maybe it was the wine.

"That was brave. I wish I could have done something like that."

"Brave or stupid, one or the other," she replied, a little embarrassed.

She muttered something about the dish she was making, which I didn't understand, and began searching in the kitchen cupboard for something.

"Have you a partner ?" I asked, sensing her loosening up more with each gulp.

At first I thought she wasn't going to reply. Then she answered hesitantly.

"I'm single. My relationship broke up when I returned from Africa."

She tugged a strand of hair behind her ear and glanced away.

"No, only me now. Me and the cats and my paintings."

There was a hint of sadness when she said it.

"I've lived a very busy life," she said pulling her hair back again, as if it was irritating her.

"Tell me about you. Tell me about Germany ? Your English is perfect. How did you learn to speak it so well ?" she asked, turning the questioning on me.

I knew the inquiry would come and I was prepared.

"My mother is German, and my father was from the UK. They meet, just after the Wall came down. He was a reporter, and my mother worked for the government. She lives in Heidelberg now. I was sent away to an international school in Switzerland."

"Sounds expensive."

"Probably, Mutti made a lot of money out of the reunification, working for the government."

"West German ?"

"One German," I said flatly. ' There is only one Germany now."

I didn't mean it, but the sentence came out coldly.

"Sorry, I do apologise." she replied.

She brushed her hair over her forehead.

"It must be have been such a relief when the Wall came down ?"

"Sort of, a lot changed. The West paid for everything and it dragged us all back down."

"Sorry ?"

"We shouldn't always celebrate the overthrow of the Communists. The State had looked after us from cradle to the grave, and now they were gone. We were lost. We felt abandoned. A lot resented the reunification, and still do. Mutti says the time in the East wasn't so bad. The Germans think those from the East are lazy and ungrateful, but Mutti says they are not. They had their dream taken away she said, and became poisoned...."

Then I realised I was telling her too much.

"Is Heidelberg your home ?" she added.

It was a strange question. I'd not thought about it before.

"Yes. Yes, I suppose it is ."

She took another swig from the wineglass.

"Do you mind me asking about your finger."

Ahh, it was the same question, which I'd answered a thousand times, all with the same response.

"Mutti, says it never formed properly, and they had to operate on it when I was little, to straighten it."

"Does it bother you ?"

"Not as much as it bothers other people. People don't like imperfection do they ? Mutti always said a diamond with a flaw was better than a pebble without."

She didn't reply, and looked upset again, and went to stir the pot.

"It's a vegetable stew. I hope you don't mind. I don't eat meat." she said almost apologetically over her shoulder, changing the subject.

"No, of course not." I replied.

"I suppose there are not many vegetarians in Germany ?"

"No, we have vegetarians as well," I laughed, " , but they are rather hungry."

"Why are you a vegetarian ?"

She then turned and put her spatula down, and looked at me with a perplexed expression.

"Do you know what, I've actually forgotten. It was forty odd years ago and I've forgotten the original reason. Now, it would be so alien me to eat meat, well, I couldn't. A lot of the girls down the stables think I'm crackers. They're all roast beef and roast potato, types."

"Stables ?"

Then there was a pause and I could tell from her expression that she was considering something. Then she smiled, turned down the gas to a simmer, strode over to me and took me by my hand and led me out of the kitchen. She almost dragged me along.

"This is my Equine Room. Cats aren't allowed in here," she exclaimed.

My jaw dropped as I entered the room. It was immaculate, clean, and decorated in the same hippy style. Framed around the walls were paintings—watercolours of horses. Shelves were filled with small carvings of stallions and larger equine busts.

Interspersed among them were numerous photographs of her atop a magnificent ebony gelding. The horse had shining bright eyes, eyes as dark as the bottom of a well. In all the photographs she was beaming, absolutely beaming.

"Ich bin auch ein Reiter!" I exclaimed without thinking.

"Sorry?" she replied, seemingly puzzled.

"Ich bin auch ein Reiter! I ride as well," I corrected myself.

To be honest, I was taken aback by it all. She beamed at me.

We sat down, and she shared the stories behind each picture— the long winter hacks, the names of ponies and horses no longer with her but forever captured in paint and cherished memories. She pointed to a painting of her current equine companion.

"This handsome chap is my current friend, Mr. D," she said.

"Mr. D?" I repeated.

"Mr. Darcy, from *Pride and Prejudice*. You know, Jane Austen?" she explained.

"Mr. D," I echoed.

Suddenly, it was her turn to get excited.

"You must come and meet Mr. D and ride him if you'd like."

He sounded marvellous. I sat there, staring at the painting, captivated by each brush-stroke. Mr. Darcy looked truly magnificent—ears pricked, nostrils flared, and coat gleaming in the winter sun. In the painting, great plumes of steam billowed into the cold morning air. I couldn't decide which was more impressive—the painting itself or the horse it had depicted.

In that moment, everything else faded away. I was once again a little girl.

We talked for hours, so much so that the vegetable stew was forgotten and turned into a crisp. I felt ashamed to admit it, but I was incredibly comfortable in her presence. It was confusing, especially when she delved into subjects that were best kept secret.

"Sadly, owning a horse just burns money. I don't know what it's like in Germany, but here..." she trailed off.

"I know," I interjected. "When I was in medical school, it was tough, but I had a little side income. It helped me through university and paid for the stabling."

"Oh, what was that?" she asked,

I felt my cheeks warming; maybe I had gone too far.

"Ohh, I did some work in corporate hospitality. There is always a demand in Heidelberg for proper entertainment."

But she wasn't listening to me. She just gazed around her room and soaked up the pictures, as if she was seeing her own paintings for the first time. Then she turned and asked.

"Do you still ride much now?"

I promised myself I would never open up, but for some reason, in that moment, it all came pouring out.

"I have a chestnut stallion, Libero! He's out on loan now, but I can see him anytime," I exclaimed with excitement, then abruptly stopped. Suddenly, I felt foolish, as if I had something to prove.

"What's he like?" she asked with genuine interest.

"Ohh, he's stabled in Wiesenbach, just south of Heidelberg. He's really...how do you say? Cheeky? Ohh, I wish you could..." I began to ramble, but I stopped myself before revealing too much.

She smiled at my childish enthusiasm, and for the first time since I had met her, she looked genuinely happy. To be honest, I left feeling confused. I even had to excuse myself and go to the toilet to gather my thoughts. I was becoming so mixed up, and that wasn't like me. Mutti had always taught me to stay focused and clear-minded.

No, this was not the narrative that my mother had described. She didn't say she could be nice. She was a poisonous bitch who murdered my sister. But for the first time, I felt uncertain about it all.

**

I now divide my existence into the time before it happened, when life was filled with optimism and hope, and the period afterward when the bleakness descended. It was a darkness that really never lifted.

Certain events in life are etched into our souls, branding us, and becoming an inseparable part of our being. No matter how many times we replay the movie, the storyline remains the same.

The night she was taken was one such event.

It was the week after New Year. The house still held remnants of *Baby's First Christmas*, adorning every corner. The heating was turned up high for her, but for me, it felt stiflingly hot. I remember her drifting off in my arms, and I decided to put her down early. I recall the last time I saw her, her rosebud mouth and flushed pink cheeks, and the tiny, exaggerated yawn she did just before falling asleep.

Then I went to bed early, simultaneously worn out and uplifted by the events that every young mother experiences each day. My bed was empty, but I wasn't alone. My life felt complete. At that time, I needed no one, wanted no one. We were one.

And then she was gone.

I cannot even begin to describe, nor find words to express, how I felt in that moment when I saw her crib was empty. At first, I froze. I noticed her covers had been pulled back, and I frantically threw them into the air, as if she was hiding beneath them, even though I knew it was impossible. But in moments of panic, logic eludes us, doesn't it? A hundred implausible scenarios raced through my mind. Maybe she had escaped? Maybe she was in my bed, and I had forgotten? It could have happened. Yes, I had awoken in the night and brought her into bed with me.

But no.

The note placed on her covers proved that it wasn't so.

Nobody will ever truly know what it was like, other than me.

I remember staring, dumbfounded, out of her bedroom window. I stood there for thirty minutes, perhaps even more, paralyzed as I tried to process it all. I didn't want to read it, to see what was written. It was too obvious, too threatening. I just stared at the note, willing it not to exist.

I remember looking out at the world, seeing it through a dark waterfall. Outside, people in their cars were heading to work, old men were walking their dogs. The world was still turning. It struck me as so utterly, fucking wrong. In that moment, I understood what Auden meant by "stop all the clocks."

In any given second around the world, millions of stories of grief unfold, cancelled out by an equal measure of pure joy. The world simply continues its course. But in that moment, I couldn't understand, didn't want to understand, and couldn't begin to fathom it.

I remember pacing around her room, clenching my fists, and hyperventilating so deeply that I nearly passed out. In those agonising morning hours, as her sheets grew colder and her scent faded, I experienced every raw emotion that God has bestowed upon us.

First came denial. I remember sneaking out of her room, going downstairs, and making a cup of tea, pretending that nothing was happening, humming to myself. It was all just a dream. This couldn't be real, not happening to me. I tip-toed back up to her room, treading carefully as not to wake her.

"Morning Popette, little sleepy head," I greeted her, hoping that the outcome would be different.

But the replay was always the same. Her sheets were as cool as marble, and with each repetition, they became dirtied, soiled linen covered by the note—an instruction that told me exactly what to do and the consequences of not complying.

Next came the guilt.

I have asked myself repeatedly, interrogated myself, chastised

133

myself. What if she had slept in my room? There was enough space, for Christ's sake. The 'what ifs' and 'maybes' have played out in my mind countless times, yet they still carry a lingering impact, their pain dulled from all the replays but not yet diminished to nothingness.

The truth is, she didn't sleep with me, and in the morning, she was gone.

Then, I remember sinking into an abyss of self-pity. The sunlight disappeared, replaced by a harsh, cold winter moon. I let myself drown in a sea of tears.

I cowered in the bathroom and entertained thoughts of cutting myself. Hurting myself, bleeding myself. If I could bear the pain, would she return? That was my twisted logic. But in the end, I dropped the scissors. I wasn't even brave enough to follow through. How pathetic is that?

The last thing I remember was sliding down the wall, my back slipping against it in stuttering steps. I sat on the floor, head buried between my knees, crying, and sobbing until I was emptied of all tears. I was convinced that God hated me. I was such a terrible mother. I deserved nothing but death.

When I awoke a day later, the heavy weight of loneliness had settled onto my shoulders like a suffocating shroud. In my vomit-covered pyjamas, I just sat and waited, staring at her crib with red, puffy eyes.

Eventually, the anger came. And with it, the need for revenge.

**

It was the happiest I had been in over thirty years, seeing her, being with her. But to be honest, not being able to tell her, to hug her, to hold her tight against me spoiled it for me. It cut me deep.

I cannot fully explain the exhilaration I felt; it's a feeling I'm struggling to convey as I write with my shaking hands. It must have been so evident to her, my joy. I did my best to suppress it. I wanted to be in control.

Yes, I made foolish, thoughtless remarks. But when she saw my horse room, her expression was priceless! It was as if she was a teenager again. In that moment, it felt like she opened up, or perhaps it was just me. Maybe it was the wine. I was so overwhelmingly happy, I had to remind myself not to show it.

When she went to the bathroom, I did something regrettable. I looked in her clutch bag, not with the intention of stealing anything, of course. Anyway, I found what I needed. I quickly jotted down the details and slipped the paper into my back pocket just before she returned. As she re-entered the room, she appeared slightly perplexed. Then she smiled at me, a smile that illuminated the entire room.

And in that moment, I couldn't help but think how beautiful she was, just as I remembered. She was so incredibly beautiful.

**

"Rebecca, you are my only daughter. Bitte, for Mutti?"

I didn't know what to say, so I remained silent. My silence only seemed to anger her more.

"Do you want me to reveal everything to the world? Explain what you are?" she whispered in a threatening tone, as if interrogating someone. I knew exactly what she meant.

"Mutti, she wasn't what I expected."

Then it was my mother's turn to fall silent.

"Do the right thing, Rebecca."

And then the line went dead.

I didn't know what to do. For the first time in years, I felt alone—confused, scared, and that's not how Mutti made me.

Chapter 11

A manila envelope arrived, just as she had said it would. I tore it open and emptied its contents onto the kitchen table. Then it hit me, like a punch to the chest. It was a Polaroid photograph of her. I dropped it as if it burned my fingers.

She looked distraught; her face red as if she had been crying herself to sleep. I stroked the picture, longing for her presence, even though it was irrational to believe she could feel it.

I read the typed instructions, their text written with a fading, intermittently inked ribbon. The enormity of the task overwhelmed me. I was struck dumb by it, hollowed out inside. Day by day, in her absence, I had become a shell of a woman. She was no longer here, and with each passing day, the void grew larger, deeper, and filled with darkness—a darkness I was shocked to discover within myself.

I went through the list, sealed the envelope, and began my journey. Why did I do it? What would you have done in my place? Succumb to despair or fight?

No, I chose to fight. I fought to bring her back. A promise I had made.

**

I pressed send, and with a whooshing sound, the message was gone. All that remained was to wait. I wasn't even sure if Gus would respond or entertain my request. But he did say he would help. I needn't have worried. Within a few hours, he replied. He would help, but there was a condition: I had to call him.

I paced back and forth. How could I ask without providing him with a fuller explanation? I couldn't disclose everything yet, but I needed to know—needed to know so desperately that it consumed my thoughts.

With resolve, I picked up the phone and dialled his number.

He answered on the first ring.

"Look, K, I'll call a few favours for this. A mate owes me quite a few drinks," he began.

"Thanks, but I'm desperate to know," I replied.

"Okay, but just so you're aware, I don't do this every day. I could get a friend fired or worse. This is a one-time favour for you. Because..."

He didn't need to explain further.

"Thanks, I appreciate it. I don't want him to get fired, but it's important." I said.

"Her. She's a woman. There are female intelligence officers these days, you know. It is the twenty-first century,"

"Sorry," I replied.

"I put her husband back together in Bosnia. Not that I expected any favours," he continued.

"Sorry, Gus."

He didn't respond, so I asked.

"I want to know who she is."

"K, before I tell you, why don't you share who you think she is?"

I pondered for a moment.

"She's German, around my age. That's all I know. I need to meet her."

"Well, using GCHQ is a bit excessive to arrange a cosy chat with a long-lost friend," he remarked.

"There won't be a cosy chat."

"Okay..."

"What do you need?" I asked.

"I just need to know her address, telephone number, email—anything like that. The rest would be a bonus."

As he uttered those words, his accent still had a way of captivating me.

Two days later he returned the call.

"What have you got?" I asked, desperate to know.

"Well," he hesitated, "her name is Ingrid Mueller. She's fifty-one years old and lives in Heidelberg. She runs a small advertising business in the city. She was previously married to an English journalist. She has one adopted daughter, Rebecca."

Gus continued, "She has quite a colourful past, by all accounts."

I suspected what he meant by colourful.

"...and another daughter who passed away when she was twelve months old."

A photo arrived in my inbox with a ping.

"Here is picture of Ingrid Mueller."

I opened it.

She looked older than I had expected. But it was her from that morning on the common. The likeness was unmistakable.

"You could have found this information through a simple internet search," Gus remarked.

"But you didn't find anything, did you?"

"No, nothing," I admitted.

"That's because Frau Mueller has been very careful. Her digital trail is virtually cold. It's quite difficult to achieve that these days, almost impossible, unless someone doesn't want to be found, or..."

"Or?"

"Or someone is helping her."

"Ingrid Mueller has a very dubious past," Gus explained.

"Stasi." he said bluntly.

"Stasi?"

"The Stasi were the secret police in the former East Germany. After the fall of the Berlin Wall, she was assigned to Project Crimson. It was the Stasi's attempt to silence their West German agents after reunification, before they could divulge any secrets."

"Silence?" I pressed.

Gus didn't elaborate.

"After all the records were made public, as part of the reunification deal, her file was officially closed, and she became inactive."

Silent, I absorbed it all.

"Kirstie, this woman is extremely dangerous and still under surveillance by the German government," Gus warned.

"Shit."

"K, stay away from her. Please?" he pleaded.

With that piece of advice, we concluded our conversation. I hung up the phone.

Staring at her photo on the screen, a grin crept across my face.

"I've nearly got you. You bitch."

But I still didn't know the crime I was being punished for.

So there was only one way to find out.

Ask her.

**

What still haunts me, even after witnessing the brutality in Rwanda, was the panic and pain in her eyes, along with her burning desire to die. She was the first child in my career who was dying before me, or more accurately, wanted to die.

Despite only being ten years old, Tilly, was the bravest little girl I had ever met. But she still wanted it all to end.

Cancer in a child made me doubt the existence of God, viewing it only as a concept concocted by men for their selfish needs to control women. The death of a child just defies the natural order of events, a tragic winter's tale.

She looked so fragile before me, as if teetering on the edge of life itself, which she was. Her parents had been deprived of sleep for weeks, their bloodshot eyes fixated on her bedside, watching her drift in and out of consciousness. They sat there, utterly helpless, while their only child winced in pain. Yet, against all odds, she resurfaced, gasping for air with rigid lungs, and continued to cling to life. I simply couldn't understand it.

The tumour on her face made it nearly impossible for her to speak, but I understood what she meant. If I knelt close and listened intently, I could just make out her words.

"Can't you make it stop?" she whispered; her voice barely audible.

I would have done the same, without hesitation.

"Look, Tilly, be brave. We'll see what we can do," I assured her.

"Please?" she pleaded, her sallow eyes fixated on me, their yellow hue the colour of mustard.

I stepped away from her bedside. Her parents looked drained, their unwavering support for her both humbling and inspiring.

Her once vibrant figure had been stripped of all fat. The tumour had drained the very essence of life from her body. The good had turned bad, and youth had transformed into old age.

"She's still a minor. Besides, you know the rules Kirstie,"

The Senior Registrar, Thomas McCloud—I recall his name—spoke without an ounce of accusation. A kind, balding man with a gentle Scottish accent, he had found himself in the same situation numerous times, his heart stretched to its emotional limits.

"I'll give her something to alleviate the pain," I replied.

He nodded gently.

"Yes, that *would* be appropriate."

I left the room and carried out the act.

The doctrine of double effect, we had hidden behind it for over two thousand years, a moral high ground disguised in the trappings of sanctimonious nonsense. The doctrine served as our shield, the secret refuge of the medical profession.

When I was just a young child, something happened that I now view with clarity. I remember that day as if it were yesterday. We were all ushered into Nana's bedroom. The curtains were drawn, and the room smelled of age and dampness. I sat there, taken aback by how frail my grandmother appeared, observing her chest rise and fall for the final time. What were the chances of me witnessing the last seconds of my grandmother's life while the family doctor stood over her, wearing a smile?

Now it was my turn. I couldn't administer a lethal dose. That would be murder, or at least assisted suicide. However, I could provide a dose to manage her pain. If, by chance, she passed away as an unintended consequence, so be it. That was the perverted logic of the doctrine.

I returned the next day, still holding on to the belief that Tilly would somehow still be there. Yet her bed was empty. Her room stood bare, and a cold breeze blew through the open windows. Her parents had left, and every trace of her presence had been erased. She was finally free.

I had done as she had asked, nothing more. I made photocopies of her notes to send off and felt a deep sense of shame.

**

"You're doing it all wrong. Your hands are too tense," he chastised.

I couldn't locate the source of the voice. Looking down from Mr. D, there was no one around. Kirstie had gone to speak with someone on the other side of the yard, leaving me alone, alone on her horse.

"I said you're doing it all wrong. For fuck's sake!"

And then suddenly there he was, looking up at me.

He grabbed the reins from my hands, loosened them, and handed them back.

"See, that way you'll have more control, and for heaven's sake, relax!" he instructed.

I was incredibly angry.

"Have you ever been on a horse before?" he inquired.

That was it. I nearly exploded but managed to restrain myself from swearing at him in German.

"Wills, leave her alone, for Christ's sake!" Kirstie interjected, returning.

"Sorry. Are you a novice?" he asked, staring up at me.

I was nearly bursting.

Then I saw his deep, brown eyes. My word, they were remarkably brown. He flicked his fringe from his forehead. He was solidly built, as if he played rugby—poorly. The bridge of his nose looked as though it had been broken and improperly set. Upon catching my gaze, he stared at the ground and took a step back. Mr. D acted as nervous as I felt, tiptoeing on his hooves.

"There, that's better, isn't it? Tidy," he continued, his voice softening.

"I ride back in Germany. I have a horse," I blurted out, then immediately regretted trying to justify myself to him.

"Tidy," he repeated and lightly smacked Mr. D on his buttock, causing the animal to startle. Then he turned and strode off, but not before smiling—I was certain he winked at me!

"Who was that rude man?"

"That's Wills. He's the vet. He spends a lot of time down here with his horses," Kirstie replied.

Kirstie didn't say anything more, but I could read her mind.

"Don't mind him. He's nice. He's been through a lot lately."

"He's got a strange accent," I commented.

"Oh, he's from the valleys," she clarified.

"Valleys?"

"Welsh."

Calming down, I stroked Mr. D's mane.

"How long have you had him?" I inquired, patting the horse's neck.

"Five years. He's a failed police horse. A bit too skittish for dealing with riots and football hooligans, but deep down, he's a big softy."

He was magnificent. His coat gleamed as if it had been polished, and he had kind, liquid eyes the colour of the deepest conker brown.

That afternoon, we rode down to the beachhead, following a worn, tattered bridleway, and watched the waves crash onto the shore. In the distance, I could make out Brownsea Island. I think that's what she called it. A gentle breeze wafted off the water. It felt so calm and peaceful. Suddenly, I realised I had missed the sea without even knowing I needed it. We stood on the headland, gazing out at the horizon, saying nothing as our horses nibbled at the grass beside us.

"You can ride Mr. D whenever you want. I'll appreciate the help," she offered, touching my arm gently.

"Thanks."

"Or should I say, tidy?" I responded, conscious of my English. She laughed, although I hadn't intended it to be funny.

She was kind. And that kindness left me feeling confused.

Reflecting on it now, those following months completely transformed everything. Kirstie would invite me to her place for drinks and meals so frequently that it became the norm rather than the exception. I'm not sure how it happened—perhaps it occurred so gradually that I didn't even notice—but I slowly became so comfortable in her presence that I could sense her absence.

I began to witness aspects of her that puzzled me. She gave without taking, an unfamiliar concept to me. She even attempted to teach me to paint when I visited. I wasn't particularly skilled, but I loved learning about watercolours, glazes, and the intricate beauty that light can possess, if only I had bothered to notice. And she gave me something even more significant than that. It was a priceless gift she helped me uncover—a gift buried deep within me.

Love.

That summer, I visited the stables most days, just before morning surgery. Sometimes, I would ride Mr. D, while other times I would simply spend time with him. I would brush him in his stable and speak to him in German, as if he understood, attempting to explain all my troubles.

Wills often showed up. He would come and tease me, calling me "Frauline" as a joke. I would refer to him as "Mr. Wills" in return. He always had a cheerful word and advice on what I should or shouldn't do. Some mornings, he would assist me in brushing

Mr. D or cleaning his stall.

But I still didn't understand.

Then, one morning, something occurred that changed everything. It was the turning point.

Mr. D was restless, bouncing around the yard. I couldn't seem to calm him down. His coat was drenched, and he was incredibly agitated. All I could hear was Will shouting at me and the echoing sound of hooves on the cobblestones, growing louder and louder.

"Quick, get him over here!" he shouted.

"I'm trying!"

Wills held the horse steady as I attempted once more to dismount using the mounting block. Mr D could sense I was getting stressed. This only made him more agitated.

The sound of his hooves grew louder and faster.

I scowled at Wills. He simply didn't understand, did he? I had done this many times before, far more times than him, that foolish British man.

"Why don't you just let me get off!" I screamed.

But it was too late.

I fell off.

I felt myself falling but remained attached by one stirrup. In truth, looking back now, I panicked.

But he caught me. Wills caught me just in time—or just barely.

I crashed to the ground, dislodging my riding hat in the process.

I stood there with my hair dishevelled, covered in horse manure.

Strangely, I felt both angry and relieved. Mr. D immediately calmed down. I was convinced he was laughing at me, that silly horse.

I didn't know what to say. I couldn't even look Wills in the eye. I felt my breath quicken suddenly.

"Sorry. That wasn't the most ladylike dismount ever," I mumbled.

Then I recall him reaching towards me, gently tucking a stray lock of my hair behind my ear. It was as if it was the most natural thing in the world to him, as if he had done it a thousand times.

My face flushed.

"Entschuldigung. Ich errötete," I stammered.

"Sorry. I'm blushing. I never blush."

I'm never embarrassed, ever. Because. But for the first time, I felt my cheeks on fire.

He simply stared at me, as if I were mad. Then he said it.

"While mantling on the maiden's cheek, young roses kindled into thought."

"Sorry?" I said, perplexed.

"Thomas Moore," he replied, then looked away, just as embarrassed as I was.

We just stood there, not knowing what to say. It was, as you say in English, a 'something and a nothing.'

In that moment, I knew he loved me, and I loved him.

Some days I'd get to the stables and he wouldn't be there, and then I knew what was happening. I felt low and for the first time I realised I was falling in love, for the first time ever. But there was nothing I could do. I felt exhilarated and trapped in equal amounts.

I still had to do what Mutti wanted: punish her.

I was so confused.

**

"Kirstie, Yes, I'm ready. It's been nearly two years now. I can't stay in a hole all my life," he stated resolutely.

I felt a mix of happiness for him and concern.

"Wills, be gentle; she's important to me," I cautioned.

In the background I could hear the stables coming alive with clatters, and the cockerel beginning its morning ritual, awakening the world.

"Have you told her?" I inquired.

There was a pause.

"No. I don't want to be seen as a sad case,"

"She needs to know, Will," I insisted.

"How are you?" he asked, changing the subject.

"Could be better, but could be worse," I replied.

"Look, she needs to know," I urged.

I sensed him pondering it.

"Okay, I'll tell her on the first date, if I get that far," he conceded.

"Oh, I'm sure you'll get that far," I teased. "You may not get a home run, but you'll get to first base."

"But don't hurt her, Wills. Please," I pleaded.

"I know about hurt, Kirstie," he responded, his voice void of bitterness.

After he ended the call, I sat on the edge of my bed, surrounded by my cats, smiling to myself. Could it get any better? Was it really coming to an end? There was only one more task left to complete.

**

I could sense her anger even before she spoke on the phone. There was a brief pause in her voice, as if she were suppressing something before each word.

"Mutti, I've been busy. Very busy," I began.

Then she started.

"Too busy to ring your mother? You ungrateful little child," she spat into the mouthpiece.

"Sorry, Mutti, but..."

"But NOTHING!"

"But..."

I nearly said it.

"I've met somebody."

But I couldn't. I was too afraid, terrified of my own mother.

"You have a job to do. You are horrible, disgusting excuse for a daughter," she hissed.

I ended the call, trembling. I would do it. Of course, I would do it. But I also knew what I wanted, perhaps for the first time in my life.

"I want to be ME!" I screamed.

But nobody could hear.

I desperately wanted to tell her, but I couldn't go through with it.

Wills had asked me out. I remember he was practically trembling when he did it. He slipped it into our conversation as we prepared the horses, almost casually. It caught me off guard.

"Mr. Wills, are you asking me out?" I asked, surprised.

"Sort of," he responded.

Years later, he confessed that he nearly fainted at that moment. I had never seen such a wide smile on a man's face before. It lit up like a child's on Christmas morning.

So, to hell with my Mutti, I said, "Yes."

"Well, Mr. Wills, I'd love to," I said.

And I truly did.

My mother could go to fucking hell.

Chapter 12

Five years after receiving the last envelope, I received another. I had no clue how she had found me. I had returned to the UK and transitioned from locum jobs to short-term hospital contracts, constantly chasing my tail and my future. But Rebecca was never far from my thoughts.

I was training to become a GP, hoping to finally settle down— well, that was the plan. One bleak afternoon, the parcel landed on the doormat. As soon as I saw the familiar lettering, I knew what it was.

It was two days before I plucked up the courage to open it. I kept it on the mantelpiece, out of reach from the cats. But after three days, I gave in. I needed to know.

I remember ripping open the bubble-wrapped package. Inside, there was only a single slip of paper with the words *"A present."* scrawled in German... and a video-cassette.

Two days later, on a Sunday evening, I closed the living room curtains and poured myself a rare drink—for that time, at least. My hands trembled as I inserted the cassette into the video record-er. Huddled on the sofa, clutching Molly tightly, I began to watch.

Initially, the picture was grey and flickering. I had braced my-self for what was to come, but I wasn't prepared for this.

On the screen was a little girl shouting "Mummy" in German. She was nearly five years old now, no longer a toddler. A bearded man held her in his arms; he appeared kind. In the background, a hillside vista swept past, on what seemed like a hot summer day. The camera was unsteady as a barge cut through the water. He playfully bounced her up and down, eliciting giggles. The images became a jumble as they swapped positions. Then there she was again, in her 'mother's' arms. The child had fiery red hair like mine used to be, with a severe haircut. I could see glimpses of my moth-er's features and the cheekbones of her father. The little girl made a face when asked to wave at the camera.

Then the woman gave her a loving, wet kiss that sent her into fits of uncontrollable giggles. It was unbearable for me to watch. I closed my eyes and shut off the snapshot of family life playing out before me.

A roller coaster of emotions hit me—relief that she was still alive, followed by sadness, despair, and ultimately, pure, unadulterated rage. If she intended to break me, it was not going to fucking work. I wanted to burst into tears, collapse on the carpet, and just hold my cats. But I didn't. Instead, it only strengthened my resolve.

I had changed.

What astounds me today is the stark contrast between who I am now and who I was just years ago. In my younger days, happiness was my constant companion, but now I find myself plagued by torment. Gone are the carefree and happy moments spent with my friends during my university years. Life has hardened me.

Change is inevitable. The world has a way of moulding us, whether we embrace it or not. Yet, importantly, our past doesn't define our future. There remains a glimmer of hope for brighter days to come. We have the power to transform and evolve. In that realisation lies eternal hope; the hope I clung to.

So I pressed ' Record ' and bleached my daughter away with the evening news, and she was gone.

I kept going because that was all I had.

**

For the first time in my life, I didn't know what to wear. He wasn't a client; he was smart and sexy, and I didn't want to come across as slutty. No, I liked him too much for that. After an hour of deliberation, I settled on a little black skirt, a cream blouse, and knee-length Italian handmade boots instead of heels. I was brimming with excitement as I stepped out of the shower and got dressed.

Finally, I was ready.

My hair cascaded in spiralling locks, and I applied minimal makeup. Standing before the full-length mirror, my hands shook with nerves. I whispered to myself, "He's just another man. Just another one of them."

But deep down, I knew he was different. Wills was so different.

I poured myself a small aperitif, trying to calm my nerves. I sat and waited.

He had said seven o'clock.

At quarter-past seven, annoyance started to creep in. By half-past, I paced the room, fuming at the unpunctuality of the typical British man.

And then the doorbell rang.

I flung the door open, ready to give him a piece of my mind about his lateness and the importance of manners.

There he stood, in dirty dungarees covered in what could only be described as mucus. He smelled like an unclean cow-pit that hadn't been tended in a month.

"Keep your knickers on, Frauline. I'm only a bit late. Had a surprise birthing to do. What was I supposed to do? Ask the poor girl to cross her legs?"

"Wills, you look a mess, and you smell rather..." I trailed off.

"...like a cowpat. Sorry, it's the placenta. Bloody stinks, that," he explained, glancing at his soiled clothes before looking back at me.

"But you look good enough to eat, and I'm starving! Wow! Nice boots, mind," he pointed at my footwear.

"Cheeky bloody man," was my first thought, but he made me laugh. So, I just scowled at him.

"I'm going to have to go home and get showered and changed. Unless you want me to go out like this?"

I shook my head, not saying a word.

"You can wait at my place. I'll only be twenty minutes. Shit, shave, shower, and I'll be good as ready."

"Too much information, Mr. Wills," I replied, smiling. "But yes, I'll come."

"Tidy."

And so, we were off.

Thankfully, he had the foresight to cover the passenger seat of his Land-Rover with a cotton sheet to protect my dress. His thoughtfulness touched me, and as we travelled to his house, I started to calm down. However, the stench still lingered around him. I shot him a disapproving look, and he seemed to be aware of it.

"Fresh air is what we need," he shouted, rolling down his window.

The cold night air rushed in, blowing my carefully styled hair in all directions. I frowned at him again, but he paid no attention.

I sat in my seat, shivering, as the car drove down a winding, rutted track away from the main road. It felt like an eternity, and just when I thought we had arrived, the vehicle changed direction, continuing deeper into the darkness.

Finally, we reached our destination. Without hesitation, he leapt out of the car as soon as it stopped and hurried around to open the door for me. I almost stumbled out of the Land-Rover.

"Here at last," he exclaimed.

I gave him another frown.

Leading the way, he took me into his house.

To be honest I had no idea what to expect, but I was blown away.

"Wow," was all I could manage when I entered.

"Yes, it's nice, isn't it?" he replied proudly.

"Wunderbar!" I exclaimed, completely taken aback by what I saw.

The house was a converted barn, weather-worn but functioning from the outside. But inside, it was an entirely different story. I almost thought it was a trick. The interior was exquisitely designed and crafted. The floors consisted of interlocking burnt oak panels, polished to perfection. In the corner of the lower floor, a sweeping spiral oak staircase led to a gorgeous open-space living room that seamlessly merged into a tastefully decorated kitchen. A polished stainless-steel island gleamed like a freshly poured mirror in the centre of the kitchen.

"Who designed this?" I asked, amazed.

"I did," he replied.

"I've only just finished renovating it. Started five years ago, but only just managed to finish it. It consumed all my time, but I suppose that's what I needed,"

"Wow," I repeated, still in shock.

"Take your shoes off," he said, growing more animated.

"Oh, I'm sorry. How rude of me." I apologised.

"It's not that. Just take your shoes off, please."

I slipped off my boots.

"Well, they're boots anyway," I corrected him.

"Whatever."

"See? Underfloor heating. Every home should have it. A real pig to install, though,"

As I walked, I could feel the warmth of the floor radiating through the soles of my feet, akin to walking on a warm beach in summer.

"If you sit on the floor with your bare arse, you'll get a nice warm red bum as well," he said, winking mischievously.

"Thank you, but I won't be trying that."

"Maybe later. The night is young!" he teased, charging up the stairs, leaving a trail of cow stench behind him.

"Help yourself to some wine. It's in the fridge," he called down.

And so, I did.

I drank the remaining contents of a supermarket bottle and surveyed the living room. The walls and shelves were tastefully adorned with pictures, paintings, and objects that clearly held great meaning to him: a signed rugby ball and shirt, countless photos of his spirited horse, and a picture of his graduation. In one photograph, Wills stood beside what I assumed were his beaming parents. They looked so proud. At that moment, I felt an overwhelming sense of happiness. I felt privileged that he had allowed me into his personal world. He was so funny, effortlessly so.

Then, my eyes saw it.

Everything changed.

There, inconspicuously placed on a table, was a small, cheaply framed photograph. The scene depicted a couple on a beach. He was laughing, with his arm wrapped around her. Her head rested against his shoulder in a tender moment captured in time. Seeing it felt like a punch to the stomach. I couldn't find my voice. I stood there, transfixed by the image, oblivious to the passage of time. I didn't even hear him come back down the stairs until he touched my shoulder. I flinched but didn't turn around.

"Who is she?" I asked, my tone stern.

"Sorry, this is all a bit awkward," he stammered.

"I said, who is she?" I repeated.

After a pause, he finally answered, "She's my wife."

I felt my insides crumble, but I shook my head and tried not to show it.

"I assumed Kirstie had told you. Apparently not," he said, lying blatantly. I could tell. Maybe he was just like all the others.

Silence filled the room, pressing down on us. Then suddenly I could hear Wills sobbing behind me, his head bobbing up and down in the reflection. I desperately wanted to turn around, but fear held me back.

"Rosie *was* my wife," he said, his voice trembling with emotion.

"She died two years ago."

"She was in a car crash while pulling the horse-box. Some idiot pulled out in front of her in the dark. The box flipped over. The horse survived... but she didn't."

I didn't know what to say. All I could see was his crumbling face reflected in the photograph opposite me.

"God, I'm sorry," I replied, covering my mouth with my hand, as if it could offer any solace.

The silence persisted, and I could hear Wills struggling to hold back tears behind me. He trembled and shook.

"She was carrying our baby..." his voice trailed off.

I couldn't bear it any longer. I turned around and hugged him with all the strength I could muster. I held him as if each embrace could mend the pain.

"Sorry," he spluttered, regaining his composure.

"Not the best start to my first date in years."

I didn't say anything because I couldn't find the words.

We stood together for a few moments, with me clinging to him. Finally, I had to break the silence

"Can I put my shoes back on?" I whispered.

"Them's boots, Frauline, not shoes," he whispered back into my ear, his touch gentle enough to send tingles down my spine.

Then, I felt his chest rise and fall against mine as we both burst into laughter, tears streaming down his face. He felt so warm and vulnerable, and I didn't know what to do, except hold him tight.

In a strange way, I was relieved that he wasn't married. As we headed to the restaurant, I felt a pang of shame for even thinking it. I've never felt shame before.

**

"'Starter?" he asked.

"Sorry?"

"Are you having a starter? I think we should push the boat out."

"Sorry, Mr. Wills, but you've completely lost me."

"Push the boat out. It's an English saying, to go all the way. Shall we have a starter, main, pudding, the whole shebang?"

"Wills, you're talking nonsense."

"Sorry, I'm getting carried away."

"Okay, I'll have the fried mushrooms if we're pushing the ship out."

"Boat." he corrected.

"Boat, then."

"How far are we pushing this boat out?" I asked.

"Probably up to our ankles, though not above our wellies."

I laughed.

"Wills, you're so silly at times."

"All the time," he replied. "Silly keeps me sane."

"Albern," I said, "Albern is German for silly."

"Ich bin Albern," he replied in his best German.

I laughed again.

"This is a strange restaurant," I remarked, looking around.

The restaurant resembled an old English tavern, or at least what I imagined one would look like. It had low wooden beams that Wills had already knocked his head on once. It had all the elements I expected: a roaring fire, red-nosed gentlemen teetering on bar stools arguing about immigrants, and a dimly lit interior that no amount of light could brighten.

"It's a gastropub," he stated.

"What?"

"A gastro-pub. A gastronomical pub."

"You've just made that word up."

I gave him a quizzical look.

"No, I didn't. It's a real word. Anyway, I don't need English lessons from a German."

"I'm half German."

"This restaurant has won awards. The chef has two Michelin stars. They even serve chips, proper ones. Just like Mam's," he said proudly.

I giggled. I could see that his eyes still glistened, but as the evening went on, he returned to the Wills I knew: witty, confident, and someone who hung on my every word.

That night, I talked about my family back in Germany. Not in detail, of course, but I felt at ease. Why? I couldn't say, but I just felt comfortable. He shared a brief history of Wales and explained why he believed it was 'God's Country'. For the first time since leaving university, I laughed. I genuinely laughed. In that moment, I was so happy, even though it was strange.

The food was fantastic—wholesome and reminiscent of Bavaria, the kind of food you crave after an afternoon of hiking in the hills: sausages in gravy with mashed potatoes and slow-cooked lamb shanks.

And then, as always, the question came. It always came. Right on cue, after a few glasses of wine, he asked it.

"What happened to the end of your finger?"

I gave him the same rehearsed response, which he absorbed without blinking.

"Does it bother you?" he asked after I finished my well-practiced spiel.

"Not as much as it bothers other people," I replied automatically, the words coming out coldly.

"Sorry," he responded, clearly upset that he had irritated me.

"No, don't be silly," I reassured him. "No, it only bothers me when I play the violin."

"Jesus! You play the violin?"

"No, because of my poorly little finger," I retorted, offering him an obscene gesture with my digit.

Wills roared with laughter, taking it as the joke it was.

The elderly men at the bar glared at us, but I smiled at them, causing them to turn away.

"And they say Germans don't have a sense of humour?"

I scowled at him.

"Yes, we do. We just laugh at different things than you do. People slipping on banana skins, getting fruit pies pushed in their faces. We find that all very funny."

"...and people getting the end of their fingers cut off," he replied coldly.

I didn't know what to say. Suddenly, I couldn't look at him.

"Sorry, I don't know what you mean?" I replied, fiddling with my napkin.

His words caught me off guard.

"The end of your finger was removed. Even I can see it."

Suddenly, the atmosphere became tense.

"Don't be silly, Wills."

For the first time, he looked away.

"What's for pudding?" I asked, changing the subject.

For a few more moments, he said nothing, as if pondering something. Then he snapped back to the present, and we were back where we were.

"Sorry?" he replied.

"Pudding?" I said softly. "...pudding?"

Will's let out a gasp and patted his stomach.

"Sorry, I'm stuffed. Though I'll share one with you," he said, changing his mind.

"Mr. Wills, for a woman, sharing a dessert with a man is one step away from..."

"...paying the bill!" he interrupted,

"Oh something else?" I replied cheekily.

He didn't reply but just sat and gawped at me.

Then banging the table laughing continued "So, I think it's a grand idea. I fancy the raspberry torte,"

The old men scowled us again. I blew them a kiss this time.

But strangely it was me that suddenly became embarrassed.

My cheeks felt burning hot. What was happening to me lately? Wills pressed the back of his hand against them in a sweet, mocking way, feeling the heat radiating from my face, which felt ablaze.

"Toasty!" he exclaimed.

"Sorry. I blush too much. I don't usually."

"It shows you care."

His words made me feel like a fraud. I had never cared about anything until now.

We shared the pudding using the same spoon.

Then I asked him.

"Why doesn't Kirstie have anybody? You know her well, Wills?"

He licked the back of the spoon and set it down, as if contemplating his answer.

"I've only known her for five years, and to be honest, nobody really knows Kirstie. She's a very private person. Anyway, she's got her cats."

"There *was* a big scandal about ten years ago, I understand. It was in the local papers," he continued.

"A scandal?"

"Apparently, she had a relationship with one of her patients. She nearly got struck off the Medical Register. I heard her defence was that the bloke had terminal cancer. Her lawyer argued that his right to love outweighed her duty not to become involved with a patient."

"Jesus!"

"She argued so eloquently during her defence that she was only given a caution. By the time the case reached the GMC, the poor chap had died, so it was all a bit academic."

"Wills, I'm quite shocked."

"She's a bit of a dark horse, our Kirstie."

"Dark horse?"

"A racehorse not known to gamblers, so it's hard to know it's true odds of winning."

And then he said it, as if an afterthought.

"I think something very bad happened to her years ago."

"Or she did something bad?" I asked, perhaps too bluntly.

He looked at me incredulously.

"What, Kirstie? She doesn't have a bad bone in her body."

From what I had experienced so far, Wills was right.

Everything I was seeing and experiencing was so different from what I had expected. I found myself in a constant state of confusion, unable to separate truth from propaganda, with Mutti's mission nagging at the back of my mind.

We finished our meal and sat staring at each other. We didn't need to say anything. We were both content, comfortable, and full—or was it just me, lost in the jumble inside my head? For once, we didn't need conversation. Wills let out a contented sigh, and I understood exactly what it meant.

As we left the restaurant, he waved and bantered with the chef about his Michelin stars and whether he could get him a new set of tyres for the Land-Rover.

Then it happened, unexpectedly. I didn't think it would catch me off guard like that.

He put my coat around me, buttoned the first button as if it were the most natural thing in the world, as if he had done it a thousand times. Then, he leaned across and kissed me.

It was a gentle kiss that brought tears to my eyes—a fleeting touch of our lips and nothing more. Then, sweetly, we pulled apart, and he kissed my forehead.

"Thank you, Frauline."

"Thank you, Mr. Wills," was all I could manage as I fought back tears.

**

"Kirstie, calm down. You're not making any bloody sense. Start again!"

I took a deep breath and tried to compose myself. The phone trembled in my hands, and my words came out in a shaky voice. Ever patient, Gus waited for me to collect my thoughts.

"I've done something bad, really bad."

I blurted out the words.

"There's nothing so bad that can't be sorted out, K. Tell me what's the matter before I jump in the bloody car and come get you."

"No, no. Please don't come."

"Then tell me."

I took a deep breath and said it.

"I've betrayed a patient's confidence."

At first, he didn't say anything. Maybe I was right. Maybe I was evil. Then he asked gently, "How, K? Tell me what happened?"

"I told them."

"Told them what?"

"I posted it on Twitter that he was HIV positive."

"Ohh..."

I could sense from his response that even Gus, who was usually unshockable, was taken aback.

"Tell me about it," he said in a soothing tone.

I started to explain, recounting the whole bloody story, leaving out the true reason why. No, I couldn't tell him that, not yet, or maybe never. But he was the only person I could turn to.

When I finished, he asked, "Does the rest of the Practice know?"

"No, this only blew up on Friday. The phone has been ringing off the hook all weekend. I even had some bloody reporter from the local news station banging on my door."

Gus remained silent for a moment.

"I'm more shocked that you even know how to use Twitter, K."

"Sorry, I was drunk," was all I could say.

It was at least half true.

Chapter 13

The sunbeam traced its way slowly across the wall as the sun rose. I moved a little closer to him, and our bare bottoms touched. He was snoring like a little pig, his mouth pulling in big gasps of air. The poor man was exhausted, poor lamb. He probably wasn't used to it. I turned around and lay there watching his chest rise and fall under the blanket. I had an urge to lean over and kiss him, so I did.

Then suddenly his alarm went off, loud enough to wake up the entire country. With the clatter of the bell and me leaning over him, he freaked out.

"Jesus fucking CHRIST!" he screamed.

In an instant, he had the look of a man who was scared witless. So, I kissed him again.

"Wills, it's me,"

"It's me, Rebecca!"

It was like seeing a drunk man coming around: first a fog, then as the mist evaporated, the realisation of what was happening.

"Yes... yes, sorry," he muttered.

"Sorry, I've always been a deep sleeper," he mumbled and ruffled his hair with one hand, which I found so sexy.

"You must be very tired," I said with a smirk.

"Yes," he replied, "too much pudding and..."

He didn't need to finish his sentence. My clothes were scattered over the floor, leading all the way back to his front door, or more accurately, his car.

"Yes, it's all coming back in technicolour detail," he said, taking a pause as the images returned and screwing up his forehead.

Wills looked into my eyes.

"Wow!"

"Wow, thanks," he said, his face filled with wonder.

"You paid for the meal," I replied, kissing him on the forehead.

As soon as I said it, I knew it came out wrong. Maybe it was my poor English.

He looked embarrassed.

"It was only a bar meal. A thank-you would have been alright, or even a little card sent afterwards."

"Wills, it was a gastro-meal," I said, smiling.

"Well, that's just great," he said, deflated.

"No, you stupid man. It wasn't because of that..."

My little boy was lost.

"...Wills, I like you, and, umm, well... I just wanted to have mind-blowing fuck with a British man," I replied, fluttering my eyelashes.

I felt him flinch as I said it.

"Sorry, we German girls like sex."

He just sat and gawped at me.

"Now, go and find me a t-shirt. I've got nothing to wear," I continued, giving him a cross look.

My poor boy didn't know what to do, then energised he leapt off the bed.

"No problem! Champion!"

Then he realised he was stark naked and looked extremely embarrassed as he hurriedly left the bedroom for the toilet, holding himself.

"Gotta pee first!"

I laughed, rolled over, and smelled where he had slept. It had a musky scent, the smell of a sweaty man, a good man. Not the scent of a man who would leave me money afterwards. Maybe I had found the one, or he had found me. I didn't know. All I knew was that I felt so incredibly happy.

Twenty minutes later, he burst back into the bedroom, holding a tray in his shaking hands.

"Ta-da! Breakfast in bed."

I was touched. It was the first time a man had ever made me breakfast in bed. Usually, they didn't do that, well, not afterward. Usually, they just go.

"Wills, that's lovely... I'm so..."

"There we are two boiled eggs and soldiers."

164

He placed the tray between my knees, and then, upon noticing my exposed breasts, he rushed off to dig in his wardrobe.

"Of course, the t-shirt. It was at the top of my list."

"Sorry, Wills, they look like slices of toast with butter on?" I asked.

"No, they're soldiers," he replied, digging through the mountain of clothes. He turned around, slightly upset that I was questioning his culinary interpretation of sliced, buttered toast. Instantly, his eyes migrated to my bare chest.

"Welsh Fusilier soldiers, they are. Ready for battle!" he exclaimed, punching the air.

"Thank you, Wills. It's very sweet. What are you having?" I asked as he threw me a t-shirt, obviously a rugby one.

I slipped it on. I don't think it had been washed, but it smelled like him, which was good.

"Oh, I'll just have some of yours. I'm starving," he said.

"Ohh, you will be. You've been a very busy boy."

He began to blush and looked away.

We sat in bed eating, saying nothing. All I could do was sit there and gaze at him.

"What did you mean about a 'home run' last night?" I finally asked, breaking the silence.

"Sorry?"

"You mumbled it as you fell asleep."

"Nothing, it's a basketball thing," he replied, lying.

"Don't you mean baseball?"

"Of course, that's what I meant."

"Umm..."

"Well, that's very interesting, Mr. Wills, as I looked up the phrase on your iPad when you were downstairs, eager as I am to deepen my English understanding."

Suddenly, I could see the blood drain from his face.

"According to the Urban Dictionary website, which was very helpful: *Home Run - To accelerate through First base-French kissing; Second base -heavy petting; Third base-oral sex and finally*

165

coming around to a Home Run - full sexual intercourse."

Wills turned beetroot red.

"I would have settled for first base, but as a Welshman, when I see the try line, I gotta go for it! And then go for the conversion!"

"Wills, I haven't a clue what you are talking about," I replied, laughing.

"That's because you're not Welsh."

He looked away again, clearly embarrassed. It was so sweet. He could be a man and a small boy at the same time. I just couldn't understand it. I could still smell the sweat on him. I placed my hand on his crotch, and instantly, I felt him getting aroused.

But it was unfair to tease him, so I stopped myself.

"What are you doing today?" I asked, changing the subject.

He thought it over for a few moments and took the last piece of my toast.

"Well, today, I'll be milking some cows," he answered in a drawling farmer's accent.

"Wills, you're a vet."

"Well, today, I'll be inseminating some German cows," he replied in the same silly voice.

I stared at him. Then he realised what he had just said, and we both burst out laughing, laughing so much that I spilled his eggs over the bedspread.

"Stupid Mr. Welshman!"

"Mad German Dr. Woman," he replied and kissed me. It was so delicious. I could still smell myself on his face and lips.

We gazed at each other again. It was so surreal.

"And your day?" he asked.

I thought it through.

"Well, today, I will tell fat people to lose weight and take some exercise; people who smoke, to quit; people with aches and pains to go home and rest, and people who come and tell me they can't cope, I'll prescribe them antidepressants. I might see a few genuinely interesting cases, but usually, they go straight to A&E, as it probably takes them two weeks to get an appointment to see me."

"Modern Britain, or what?" he replied.

"So why did you come to the UK?"

The question caught me off guard as I remembered why I was here.

"Because I have a job to do," I replied ambiguously.

We sat in bed surrounded by crumpled, stained sheets that were still damp from the night before, staring at each other.

He finished off the last of my breakfast.

"Do you think we've got time for, well, a rematch?" he said sheepishly.

I pulled him towards me.

"If we don't try, then we'll never know?"

"How very German," he replied.

That morning, I was very late for work, and I'm not sure Wills even made it to his farm. But we both enjoyed it. It was good to feel him inside me again, a good man inside me, for once.

**

"Can you tell me why Dr. Bowen-Wright released the information? I understand that Mr. James is going to sue?"

I had no idea what the hell was going on. Outside the Surgery, the car park was packed. I gave the journalist a glare, but she only repeated her question.

"Es tut mir leid, aber ich weiß nicht, was du redest," I replied and barged my way through, much to her anger.

Given the hour and the chaos outside, the waiting room was practically empty. Usually, at that hour, it was a deafening, crowded mass of sick and elderly patients. Today, it was almost deserted. Something was wrong.

Carol, the receptionist, frowned as soon as I entered.

"Didn't you get the message?"

"Sorry, my phone's been off."

In truth, I had dropped it in Wills' car last night as we ignited our chain of amorous events.

"All surgeries are now covered by locum, today and all next week, yours included. Kirstie sent a message for you not to come in."

"What the heavens is going on?"

Carol looked at me with an expression that captured the awkwardness of the moment.

"Don't you know?"

"Know what?"

"Look, it's better she tells you herself."

"Fuck," was all I could say.

I stormed out of the reception and back into the arms of the mousy-haired, podgy reporter. She looked as if she hadn't discovered makeup yet. She repeated her question. I stopped.

In anticipation, she opened her notebook.

"Sich verpissen," I replied, "and if you don't understand that, it means fuck off!"

I got in my car and raced over to speak to Kirstie, leaving the bedlam behind me.

I didn't know what the fuck was going on. I always knew what was going on. Mutti had taught me that. But now I wasn't sure of anything.

**

When I arrived, the front door was half-open.

"Kirstie? It's me, Rebecca."

I crept into the kitchen.

I found her sitting at the table, her head in her hands. Cats were milling around, but she seemed oblivious to them. She looked like she hadn't slept all weekend. The felines meowed continuously and appeared starving.

"Kirstie, are you okay?"

"Kirstie, what's the matter? I've just come from the Surgery.

168

What the hell is going on?"

She raised her head and looked at me wearily, as if it required a Herculean effort. Her eyes were bloodshot. The kitchen stank. The cat litter tray was nearly overflowing.

"I've... I've done something bad... again," she whispered, as if speaking the words was a struggle.

"Have these cats been fed?"

She didn't reply.

I began opening a tin of cat food, and instantly they rushed towards me.

"Kirstie, what's the bloody matter? Unless you tell me, I can't help."

"It's not your problem."

"It is my problem. You are my problem."

She looked up and smiled. It felt strange, even surreal.

"Thank you, but I don't know where to start."

"Start at the beginning," I replied, moving the litter tray outside before I began to feel sick.

I could see the dark circles under her eyes. She looked absolutely drained.

Then she took a deep breath, exhaled with a sigh, and began.

"I have a patient, had a patient, I should say, who is HIV positive."

"I have a few patients like that as well."

"This one is a dentist."

"Ohh."

"He's refusing to stop working. He's putting his patients in danger. I didn't know what to do."

"There's not a lot you can do," I replied.

"I did get him to tell me the names of the men he slept with. He is a rather promiscuous homosexual by all accounts, so I could at least discuss the matter with their GPs in confidence."

"And?"

"I posted his name on the internet."

"You did what?"

"And also, the names of all the men he'd had sex with."

"Mein Gott!"

I stood there in complete shock. I had done worse, for sure. But this was different. This was Kirstie. I was utterly astonished.

"The media is all over it. Some of the men were married. Even their wives didn't have a fucking clue."

"Why did you do such a bloody crazy thing?"

Her face went pale, and she didn't say anything for a few moments.

"I needed to protect his patients."

As she said those words, I knew she was lying. I didn't know why, but she was lying. She put her head back in her hands again.

"What are you going to do?" I asked, and at that moment, all I could hear was the meowing of the cats for more food and the stench of their excrement.

She raised her head again.

"Go away until it's blown over ? Or at least until the news hounds have calmed down or gone off to chase something else. Then I'll come back and probably be struck off the Medical Register, I suppose," she said with resignation in her voice.

"Surely it won't come to that?"

"Oh, it will. I've got some what we call in Britain 'previous.'"

"Previous?"

"Previous bad behaviour," she replied with a grimace. "Anyway, it doesn't matter anymore because it's the last thing I needed to do. I just want closure now."

I said nothing.

What she said reignited the conflict I was feeling, a conflict between what I could see and what Mutti had said. If it had happened months before, I wouldn't have thought much of it. It would have been yet another example of the malicious acts she could perform. But not now. I couldn't understand. So, for one of the few times in my life so far, I went with my heart.

"Where are you going, then?" I asked.

"I was booked to attend a conference in Frankfurt, on medical ethics. How fucking ironic is that? I might as well still go. It seems like a good enough excuse not to be here."

I stared at her. She looked so helpless and deflated by it all. I thought it through and didn't even hesitate to ask.

"I'll come with you. You shouldn't be alone."

Her eyes welled up as she looked at me.

"Thank you. I'd appreciate that."

"Don't worry," I replied, trying to reassure her.

Suddenly, the cats scattered everywhere as he burst into the kitchen with the awkwardness only a former rugby player could possess.

"Hello! What's going on here then? What's that bloody smell?"

"Cat shit, Wills," I replied. "If you don't recognise that, then you're not a very good vet."

"Sorry, I only deal with big animals, not pets," he protested.

I gave him a wink, which calmed him down.

"I went to the Surgery, but they sent me here. I've got your mobile phone. You must have dropped it in my car last night."

"Yes, as you were clumsily removing my bra."

The poor man's face dropped. Kirstie burst into laughter and broke into a smile, lighting up her face as if a switch had been turned on.

"Thank you, both of you. I am so glad somebody is having some fun around here."

Wills handed me my phone.

When I saw all the messages in my overflowing inbox, my heart sank.

They were from Mutti.

I'm sure neither of them noticed. Ever the chameleon with my feelings, I hid it. But instantly, I felt absolutely sick.

**

I've always despised men. My mother taught me this. And why

171

did she loathe men? My father leaving us probably was the reason, though I've never asked her. No, I was never brave enough to ask, not when I was young.

Mutti taught me how weak, pathetic, and ruled by their cocks men can be. I noticed it when I was at university, notice how they looked at me as I walked across the square. There was always a group of them outside the café, drinking in the sun, leering at me. Outwardly, they looked so restrained, but inside, I knew it was different, as they salivated at me. They were no different from my father and what he did.

Over the years, I've learned how to twist it around, exploiting their pathetic weaknesses for my needs—revenge, not just for monetary gain. No, it was also to punish them, trick them, and show that my mother and I were stronger.

"Men are worms," she used to say, "Worms, and nothing more."

One worm masturbated over me after we did it. I was only seventeen. I still remember his grunt, his contorted retching eyes, and then the hotness hitting me.

He never did it again. He couldn't. I'd never heard a man squeal like that before—the squeak of a piglet with its little tail nearly sliced off as it ran around the room, holding itself, blood trickling down its thighs. I'd never laughed so much in my life.

But now, it's so different. I'm so confused. It feels so refreshing, clean, and natural. So, I've made a conscious decision to try to explain it to her, to explain how fond I am of him, to make her understand. I need to make Mutti understand.

**

Rebecca had shaken me out of my torpor. When she agreed to come with me, I was immediately energised. All the squalor around me snapped into sharp focus. The problem with the media slipped away. I now knew what I needed to do, or should I say, had to do.

I held the worn and dishevelled folder in my hands. I inserted the last page, the page that told the truth, the undeniable truth of science over lies, truth over falsehood. I bound it in a red ribbon and sealed it. I hid it in the inner lining of the case, then packed.

**

"How is your new lover"

I was taken aback by her question. We hadn't spoken in months.

"How do you know?"

"I have my ways."

"So, how is your Mr. Wills, as you call him?"

"Mutti, how do you know?"

"Well, as they say in England, a little bird told me."

If I knew anything about my mother, it was that she was crafty, inquisitive, and determined.

"Tell me about him," she said after a pause so long I thought she had hung up the phone.

"Oh, he is so sweet, and he makes me laugh, and he rides."

I spoke the words like a lovesick, gushing schoolgirl who wanted to tell the world. I stopped myself and took a breath.

"How sweet. Rebecca, you've become like a smitten child again."

"How old are you?"

"Twenty-nine," I replied.

She didn't say anything more. She didn't need to. Mutti knew how to humiliate through silence and unspoken things.

I could hear from her breathing that she was angry—a tense string, pulled taut, about to snap.

In those moments, it was best to say nothing. I had learned this.

'Now, tell me about the job you are going to do."

"The job?"

"Yes, the task I asked you to do. I'm sure you wouldn't forget something as important as that?"

"No, Mutti."

I had almost hoped she had forgotten, ridiculous though it was.

"She's not as you said she would be. There must be some mistake. She's been kind. Something bad happened to her years ago."

My words were met with a wall of silence, but I pressed on.

"She has big problems at work. Big problems. I need to help her."

Then she exploded. My mother erupted in a blast of fury.

"Suffered? She is just a stained piece of SHIT!"

"...but...Mutti...please."

There was a tremble in her voice as she shouted the words at me.

"Because of this bitch of a woman, I have suffered. Because of her, I only have one daughter, one daughter who is nothing but a common slut, a common PROSTITUTE!"

"Mutti, please,"I whispered, but she wasn't listening.

"Do as I say," she continued, then paused.

"Unless you want the world to know your ways? I'm sure this lover of yours would like to know who he is soiling himself with his cock?"

And not for the first time in my life, she made me feel bad and empty. But I wasn't. I knew I wasn't. But I didn't say anything. I was too afraid. I just kept quiet and waited for it to pass.

Then her anger dissipated into silence as she put down the phone, and I was left with just the dial tone in my ears.

I bit my lip, trying to make it bleed. Tears trickled down my cheeks. The doorbell rang. I heard Wills outside. I was too trapped and confused to answer, so I went into my room and hid, like I used to.

**

"Wow, that would be marvellous. Really. Thank you. You've been too good."

"We can stay at my old friend's house in Wiesenbach. It's just outside Heidelberg. It's where my horse is stabled. We can ride out. It will be nice."

"I've never been to Germany."

"I'll show you."

In that moment, I was both ecstatic that Kirstie would leave early with me and disgusted with myself, ashamed of what I was going to do. I kept them separate, in different rooms in my head. Though I knew soon I'd have to open the door between them.

I had decided. I was now in silent resignation of the task ahead. Mutti always got her way. She had always hunted them down eventually, trapped them, and then they were gone. "Punishing the traitors," she used to say, "Traitors to the cause."

Then she would tick them off her list, a list pinned to our kitchen wall. Her "Einkaufszettel" or "shopping list," she called it. But she was different.

"This one is for the family," she would said.

"This one is for you and me, Rebecca, and your poor sister."

I remember when Mutti said it and gave that little smile she did, the one that brought out the crow's feet around her eyes.

I know now it was a nasty little smile, but at the time, it was just how my mother was.

Chapter 14

After nearly two hours of searching the internet and a bottle of wine, I finally located her. Once Gus provided me with the name of the town, it was relatively easy. I had gathered everything: Rebecca's workplace, her address, and even the topic of her final-year dissertation. I felt quite satisfied with my findings, so I poured myself another drink.

An additional hour passed, during which I sent all the gathered information to the agency. I even embellished the job offer, enticing her with the possibility of becoming a partner in the Practice. If that didn't catch her attention, nothing would. In the accompanying covering letter, I emphasised the importance of discretion, making it a top priority.

A few weeks later, the applications arrived in the post. I promptly discarded all, except for one.

Mutti had explicitly instructed me not to contact her. Ever.

But I didn't. She contacted to me.

**

"It's so quiet," I remarked.

As we drove down Haupstrasse, I was taken aback by how tranquil it was. On that sunny late-spring Sunday afternoon, there was little evidence of life. A few families were strolling along the nearby woodland trails, which rose steeply on both sides of the village, but apart from that, it felt eerily quiet. It reminded me of Sundays from my childhood over forty years ago in Yorkshire, when everything used to be like this.

The scene perfectly matched my image of a sleepy German village: narrow three-storey houses with steep gabled roofs, surrounded by small, well-tended kitchen gardens brimming with sprouting plants ready to burst into life in the coming months. These gardens were clearly cared for and loved. It was quaint, but not in a kitschy way. Each home had its own unique charm, yet they all fitted together in a connected style.

Everything appeared clean and orderly, as if I had stepped onto a film set. It was a systematic arrangement, but not monotonous. Each element was distinct, yet they formed a cohesive whole. It was a cliché, but a cliché that held true.

As we passed through Wiesenbach, we saw a bakery, a butcher, two churches, the resplendent Town Hall at the centre of the village, and two sets of stables. My attention was drawn to the horses, which looked well-cared for and, dare I say, expensive.

Truthfully, the village was not much different from hundreds of other villages scattered throughout Germany. These villages were protected, preserved, and cherished by their residents in their own unique ways. The suffocating grip of commercialisation, that had diminished their English counterparts, turning them into mere tourist attractions, was absent here. Wiesenbach was a village that lived and breathed, pulsating with values and traditions.

Rebecca noticed my gaze as families, equipped with walking sticks, vigorously ascended the hill.

"Hiking. We love hiking. We enjoy everything about the outdoors," she shared.

"I can see that. It's so quiet here," I replied.

"Oh, you'll see it's much busier tomorrow. Sundays in Germany are meant for family, friends, and optionally, church," she explained.

"In the UK, Sundays are often about nursing hangovers and visiting shopping centres," I replied. "We lost the essence of Sundays a long time ago."

"It's sad. When you lose something important, sometimes it's impossible to regain it," she answered.

I thought about her response before continuing the conversation.

Then I noticed a group of individuals gathered by a shop window, their presence strikingly distinct in their Eastern attire. The women had their heads covered with burkas, while the men donned flowing robes.

Rebecca noticed me looking and remarked, "They are refugees. We have many in our country now."

"I understand," I responded. "Yes, we live in an imperfect world, with imperfect solutions at times. That's what my mother used to keep saying."

"Yes, tell me about it." I added.

I noticed one of the women laughing and wondered whether it was genuine. Or was it just a mask - like my own?

"Being far away from home must be incredibly difficult. I used to work with Médecins Sans Frontières, though that was many years ago."

Rebecca shot me an uncomfortable stare.

"Yes I remember you saying" she replied before continuing.

"We are more tolerant than most countries, due to our history,"

"Yes, I wish we had that level of tolerance. It's so important," I added.

"Tolerance stems from society and upbringing, from one's family," I mused.

Rebecca remained silent, and I carried on.

"My mother passed away a few years ago. She never fully embraced the multicultural world. When I told her I was going to work in Africa, she thought I was putting my life at risk. My father wasn't any better. They weren't at all tolerant of different people. Anyone outside of Yorkshire was a foreigner to them. He lives in a care home now. He's a bit daft at times, bless him. He's completely senile now, though."

I turned to Rebecca.

"Were your parents tolerant, would you say? Is your mother a tolerant person?"

Rebecca didn't respond, but I noticed her wince. She remained silent until we reached our destination.

"Here we are, our Ferienwohnung!" Rebecca exclaimed.
I looked at her puzzled.
"Holiday home." she translated.
"Yes, it's not mine, but a friend's."

I was surprised by how new and well-maintained it looked. The exterior had been recently renovated, sporting a lime-green colour that didn't particularly appeal to me, but the tasteful decor inside made up for it. As we entered, a gust of cold air greeted us, along with a faint scent of damp laundry wafting from a ground-floor wash-room. It reminded me of a fragrance I hadn't experienced in years, the scent of laundry being drained and hung on clothes horses.

Following Rebecca, I ascended a set of marble stairs into a combined lounge and kitchen area. The setting sun cast a warm yellow glow through the kitchen blinds, bathing the interior in a cosy atmosphere. Everything was immaculate, bright, and modern.

"There are three bedrooms on the top floor. Choose whichever one you prefer," Rebecca offered, smiling.

"Thank you," I replied.

"You look tired. You need some rest. We'll go riding tomorrow morning, if you'd like."

"Yes, I'd love that," I responded.

Truth be told, I was utterly exhausted. The past few days had been quite hectic.

We spent the rest of the evening engaged in light-hearted conversation about trivial matters. I lost count of how many times she mentioned Wills' name. In between sips of wine, she would glance at her phone and smile. There was an ongoing secret conversation between them, even as we spoke.

I had mixed feelings about their relationship. On one hand, I was genuinely happy that he had found someone else—he desperately needed it. On the other hand, I harboured deep concerns that he might get hurt or become entangled in the impending storm. It seemed to be the story of my life—wherever I went, someone ended up in a mess. I had accepted this inevitable truth.

After dinner, we sat on a small veranda facing the hillside, watching as the sun slowly descended behind the ridge. Both of us were content and silent, as only a sunset, a satisfied stomach, and wine can make you. The days were on the verge of summer. In a fleeting moment, the sun vanished, leaving a soft glow along the ridge. The air suddenly chilled, and an overwhelming silence enveloped us.

That's when I noticed something peculiar—maybe it was the light.

"The trees are all different," I remarked.

"I'm sorry?" Rebecca asked.

"The trees here—they're all different."

Sprinkled across the hillside, the trees appeared randomly yet purposefully positioned in a way I had never seen before. Or perhaps it was the wine playing tricks on my eyes. Some trees were adorned with emerald leaves, while others still slumbered, and a few were already donning adolescent dresses with white and pink apple blossoms. Intermingled among them were naive saplings, eagerly awaiting their turn, a day called tomorrow. It was all so stunning, akin to a painting. A painting that, as the glow faded to darkness beyond the ridge, transformed into monochrome.

"Things can be different," she said.

"Can they?" I asked.

"I hope so," she responded.

Though she spoke more to herself than to me, I was too fatigued, or perhaps too intoxicated, to reply.

**

As we drove from the airport, my mind was consumed with thoughts of Mutti. I kept replaying the task she had assigned me, going over it again and again. I must have seemed incredibly rude as I sat in silence during the flight. Of course, Kirstie had her own worries to contend with.

One thing I noticed about her was her propensity for moments of silence, where she would become lost in her thoughts and not say a word. And then, just as suddenly, she would snap out of it and be back to her usual self, as if her worries had magically disappeared. We all have our concerns, and mine were centred around the task I was given.

I vividly remember the day Mutti told me about my sister, the sister I never knew existed. She didn't reveal the whole truth at once; she believed I wasn't ready to hear it. Finally, when I turned sixteen, she shared the details of what had happened. I felt a surge of anger, hurt, and betrayal. Perhaps that's why I am the way I am. Yes, I know I'm not normal. Not normal at all.

I had hoped that as time passed, the pain within my mother would fade. But it didn't. If anything, she stoked the embers and fuelled her hatred for the woman I was now sharing a car with. At times, I found myself sharing in her hatred, but there were moments of doubt when I wasn't so sure.

When Kirstie asked me about tolerance and Mutti, it pricked me. It nearly made me slam on the brakes, though I think I managed to hide it. By the time we arrived at the Ferienwohnung, I had regained my composure, but I still felt uncertain. It startled me, adding another thread to the growing blanket of worries I was wrapping myself in. Only my Wills kept me going.

Before I left for the airport, I knocked on his door. I had intended to say a quick hello and goodbye. In the back of my mind, I worried it might be our last meeting, forever if Mutti got her way. She always got what she wanted. He could see that I had been crying, but soon I was laughing. What should have been a brief farewell and a quick kiss turned into a passionate encounter. His pent-up passion impressed me as we made love in the hallway, something unexpected from an English—or should I say Welsh—man. They're usually too shy to express their true desires.

Afterwards, I deliberately called him a dirty English bastard, which upset him.

"I'm not bloody English!" he retorted.

He was quite sensitive about it, my 'silly bugger,' as Kirstie would say. He sent me texts all night, which was quite nice. I tried to keep up with Kirstie's conversation, but it was difficult. Perhaps she noticed, perhaps not, but I didn't care. As the night wore on, she grew increasingly tipsy, and I eventually had to help her up the stairs. She apologised profusely, but I didn't mind. It was quite amusing.

As I lay in bed, all I could think about was what Kirstie had said. Where was my dear, lovely Wills? My bed felt empty as the rain splattered against the windowpane above me. With the water tapping a staccato melody on the glass, I finally drifted off to sleep, having decided what I needed to do.

**

Rebecca introduced the horse.

"This big boy is Libero. He's big, but he's... how shall I put it? A big softy?"

"Yes, I can see he's a big softy. He's gorgeous," I replied.

The stallion instantly recognised her and became restless, pawing the ground and nearly dancing on his hooves. He was immaculate, his hazelnut coat freshly brushed and gleaming in the morning sun, resembling polished oak.

"Libero, calm down," she scolded, paying no mind to his agitation. Her reprimand only made him more excited.

We were at Die Reitschule, as she called it—a small riding complex affiliated with a local farm within walking distance of our Ferienwohnung. I had even practiced saying the word. The yard had a rectangular layout, opposite which was a ménage with oak chippings several feet deep. Adjacent to it was a small schooling pen, also meticulously maintained. Everything was just right.

Strangely, I felt oddly at home. It was early morning, shortly after sunrise, and I had a lingering headache. I rarely get headaches, so perhaps it was from traveling, or more likely from the wine last night. I think I embarrassed myself, again.

The stable yard buzzed with the sounds of chatter and gossip, but in a language I couldn't comprehend. Young girls giggled, men shouted, and people laughed. Although I couldn't understand the words, the meaning was clear. There were also little idiosyncrasies that differed from back home. Wood was everywhere—logs stacked high in latticed blocks, bags of oak chips spilling over, and haphazard arrangements of tree trunks waiting to be cut. The stable doors themselves were works of art, adorned with exquisite Gothic script and figures of galloping horses. The stables were solidly built, made 'reet-proper' as Dad would say, with a sturdy wooden structure topped with slate tiles and heavy, zinc-plated guttering that looked built to last.

Back at our farm, things were quite different. The stables were hastily assembled with breeze-blocks and covered in corrugated iron sheeting that flapped and rattled at the slightest gust of wind. Cheap plastic guttering was installed poorly and leaked from the moment it was put up. Here, everything seemed valued. There were no overflowing plastic buts catching rainwater like we had at the farm, ones that had been bleached under the sun's rays for the past twenty years. Instead, they had hardwood barrels, even varnished. It was a small detail, but it blended perfectly with the heritage of the yard. Every piece had importance here. Even the farmer's tiny two-stroke tractor, which looked like an exaggerated child's toy, had been repainted and polished until it appeared no different from the day it left the factory over fifty years ago. It had been cared for, like everything else here. It made me wonder— why couldn't we care for what was important to us before it was taken away?

"Would you like to ride him?" Rebecca asked.

"Sorry?" I responded.

"Would you like to ride Libero with me this morning?"

"Oh."

I wasn't sure. He seemed like a handful, but I could see in her eyes that the offer was genuine and an honour. Perhaps she wanted to repay the kindness she received back at the farm. I knew I couldn't refuse.

Suddenly, Rebecca's phone buzzed, and she glanced down at it as if it were an emergency. Then, a smile spread across her face.

"Wills?"

"Possibly," she replied, grinning widely.

"Send him my love."

But she paid no attention to my words, too engrossed in typing a message on her phone.

"Yes, I'd love to ride him," I finally replied.

"Wunderbar!" she exclaimed, snapping back to reality.

Then she smiled at me, looking radiant in the morning sunlight. The rays caught the red in her hair, making it glow like smouldering embers.

"There's spare tack in the yard canteen. I'm sure you can borrow some," she said, shielding her eyes from the sun.

Rebecca led me to a cabin that seemed larger on the inside than it appeared from the outside. It wasn't anything extravagant, but it had wooden tables, chairs, and a lovely, purpose-built kitchen area. As soon as I walked in, the aroma of freshly brewed coffee and warm hazelnut pastries filled the air. Back home, all we had was a portable steel cabin, the kind you see on construction sites for workers to have their tea and read tabloids away from the elements. The girls in the yard referred to it as our 'Gossip Shack'. It was rusty, cold, and leaked. Their cabin, on the other hand, was warm, clean, and inviting.

As we entered, everyone became animated upon seeing Rebecca. The air was filled with a flurry of German that was incomprehensible to me, but the gestures accompanying the words conveyed their meaning. Hugs and kisses were exchanged in the excitement of seeing a friend return. Rebecca had to practically pry herself away from them as they swarmed around her, each

185

person talking over the other in their enthusiasm. Then, one of her friends gestured towards a middle-aged woman sitting at the back of the cabin, clutching a mug of coffee. Rebecca's face dropped upon hearing what her friend said, though I couldn't make out the meaning, I could discern the tone.

A hush fell over the room.

Rebecca hurried over, and they exchanged what seemed to be insincere kisses. The woman had greying hair pulled back tightly into a ponytail. Her face was thin, her features harsh, and her crystal blue eyes piercing. Rebecca returned to me looking troubled.

As we prepared to saddle up, I tried to engage her in conversation, but she suddenly appeared distant.

"It seems like your friends missed you. They seem nice," I remarked.

"Yes, they're my only friends," she replied softly, almost to herself.

"Except for Mr. Wills," I added.

"Oh, he's not just a friend. He's more than that."

"Yes, I've noticed," I said.

"Who was that woman?" I asked.

At first, she didn't respond, but realising she had no choice, she finally told me.

"She's, my mother."

**

Why did she come? Why did she come? I was furious. How did she know I would be there?

But Mutti always knew everything. It was her way, her 'training,' as she called it. She was checking up on me. My nosy mother was spying on me. We exchanged a few harsh words, which I was glad Kirstie couldn't understand. I caught a glimpse of something passing between them. It filled me with anger, but I had to conceal it.

When Kirstie asked who she was as we walked towards the ride, I had to tell the truth.

I remember her suddenly stopping and struggling to breathe. I thought she was going to pass out.

"Are you alright?" I asked.

"Sorry, sorry, it's the pollen," she said, pointing to the blooming clematis growing nearby.

It took her a few moments to compose herself.

"Here, let me take the tack off for you."

"Thanks. Sorry. I'm better now," she replied, though she didn't look it.

So, I decided to take it easy that morning and opted for a gentle ride through the woodlands. I needed time to think it through once again.

We saddled up. She rode Libero, and I borrowed one of the horses from the riding school. Libero seemed confused. But when she mounted, I knew everything would be alright. Instantly, the tension melted away from her shoulders. Rider and horse became almost one, built on nothing more than trust.

We set off at a slow pace. I could tell it was too slow for her, but Kirstie controlled Libero magnificently. I stayed close to her as we rode into the woodland. We followed the gravel path, surrounded by trees. The sun turned into scattered rays of light piercing through the canopy above, creating a mosaic of emerald blackness. Suddenly, it was still. The only sounds were the breaking of twigs under the horses' hooves and their rhythmic breathing as we ascended towards the summit.

I contemplated what I was going to do. I had made peace with the consequences. I would do enough to satisfy her, and no more.

Eventually, we reached the top. We dismounted, tied up the horses, and let them rest.

I had forgotten how beautiful it was up there. Below, the hillside sloped down into the valley.

"That's Neckargemund," I pointed out the village straddling the river below.

"What's the river called again?"

"The Neckar."

"Are those barges?"

"Yes, you'll see them tonight. They transport coal, cars, everything."

"The river leads back to Heidelberg," I continued, "then to Mannheim in that direction, and eventually flows into the Rhine the other way."

"It's so pretty," she said, genuinely appreciating the view.

"This part is the Burgenstrasse - The Castle Road. It's a region in Germany with many castles. Here is where two German states meet. Long ago, we didn't always get along, and there was a lot of fighting."

"And now you're one big, happy German family?" she asked.

"Of course. But families still fight sometimes,"

"Why is that?" she asked, looking her in the eye.

I didn't reply.

"Have you been to Heidelberg before?" I asked, avoiding her question.

"No, never."

"I'll take you to Rossi's for dinner. It's my favourite place. It's very relaxed."

"That would be lovely,"

I could sense her mind was elsewhere again. My own thoughts were in a different place too. I had the tools, the instructions, but what was missing was the motivation. It had vanished, absent for the first time in my life.

Behind us, I could hear the horses growing restless, pawing at the ground. We saddled up and cantered back down to the stables in complete silence. All I could think about was Mutti.

Fortunately, when we returned, my mother was gone.

**

I had envisioned this moment for nearly three decades. When it finally arrived, it was over in an instant. It happened so suddenly that it almost felt anticlimactic. My hatred for her had kept me going, but not from the start. Initially, I simply managed to cope, to hold myself together. But over the years, I learned the game she was playing and played along, nothing more, nothing less.

She seemed smaller than I remembered, or perhaps it was just my imagination. Though in truth, the brief confrontation on the common that morning felt like a distant memory, and the details had faded.

When I saw her in the cabin, I didn't think much of her—a small, inconsequential, late-middle-aged woman. But when Rebecca said it was her, the truth hit me so hard that I could barely breathe. It was like something you rehearse over and over, preparing for the moment it happens, and when it does, it's over in a flash. In a way, I felt cheated.

Was I sorry for what I was about to do? No. The unanswered question still demanded an answer, and regardless of how it ended, at least I would know. Or so I hoped. I would do it tonight, in the restaurant. It had to be somewhere public, somewhere open.

When I returned to the Ferienwohnung, Rebecca was preparing lunch. I checked the folder again from my bedroom to ensure everything was still there. I could hear her singing in German, a melody that came naturally to her. She sounded so sweet.

We spent the afternoon sunbathing in the small, enclosed garden facing south, sipping on chilled white wine. The garden was filled with unfamiliar plants and large, pristine white hydrangeas, which I didn't care for. We engaged in meaningless conversation, mostly about horses for me and Wills for her. We cautiously approached the topic of the future, taking baby steps together. At that moment, we avoided discussing the past, keeping it at arm's length. The conversation became revealing and intimate as we peeled away another layer of emotions that had enveloped us. On that afternoon, we revealed a little more of ourselves.

"Shall we head into town for dinner? We can visit the castle before sunset," she suggested.

I squinted as the descending sun illuminated her red curls. I noticed a stray grey hair glistening in the light. I wanted to say something and pluck it away, but held back. Instead, I let it sway in the breeze, moving like a silver strand before me. I didn't know her well enough to mention it, to tell my own daughter that she had a grey hair. That said it all. In that moment, I hoped with every fibre of my being that one day I would. In truth, Rebecca was so close to me, yet still an eternity away.

My next step was all about creating a beginning, and hopefully making it come to an end.

Chapter 15

"It's a ruin, but it's a magnificent ruin," I exclaimed.

We stood on the balustrade of the Castle, and the view unfolded below us, overwhelming in its beauty. Heidelberg stretched out beneath, with the river tracing a ribbon along the valley floor— slow, steady, and silent. On each side, the hillside rose steeply, dotted with dwellings that gradually faded into the impenetrable pine forest. Below, the Altstadt stood, a maze of medieval dwellings built closely together over the centuries. The buildings fragmented to the west, giving way to a vista that resembled any modern German city. I could just about make out the tourists milling about on the Altbrücke, the bridge that connected the heart of the town nestled against the southern bank of the river, with the quiet pedestrian boulevard on the north.

"I suppose you've been up here many times?"

"Surprisingly, no," I replied. "This is my first time. It's funny, I'm a tourist in my own town."

"Sometimes when something is so close, you take it for granted," she said, and her words resonated with me.

Carried on a gentle evening wind, I could hear music as a cruise boat slipped under the bridge. The sounds of laughter waxed and waned on the breeze, only to fade away as the boat sailed by, leaving behind the stillness of the evening. Silence enveloped us once more. All the tourists had left the Castle grounds, and apart from an old man talking to himself on a bench, we were alone. The sun began to dim behind the hill, casting a crimson hue on the underside of the billowing clouds, painting the sky darker with each passing second and bringing a coolness to the air.

"This really is such a wondrous place. Was it ever bombed during the war?" she asked.

"No. It's been said that General Patton declared Heidelberg as his favourite city, so it was spared," I explained.

"It really is wondrous,"

And she was right. I had forgotten just how breath-taking home could be, especially after being away for so long. I tried to find the words to describe it to her, but none seemed adequate. Then, the boat dwindled to a mere speck of light on the shimmering water.

"My parents used to take me on a cruise boat along the Neckar every summer, without fail—well, until my father left," I shared.

"Where did your father go?" she asked.

"He left," I responded, not needing to elaborate further. From her look and troubled smile, I could tell she understood.

"How old were you?"

"Sixteen," I replied, glancing down at my phone partly to divert the conversation.

"No reception up here then?"

I smiled in return, grateful for the shift in topic.

"How is Wills?"

Was it that obvious? I thought to myself. "Oh, he's fine," I replied. "He mentioned that feeding your cats is an absolute nightmare."

"Well, it was kind of him to offer at such short notice,"

Then, unexpectedly, she asked me, "You love him, don't you?"

Her question caught me off guard. At first, I didn't know how to respond. It felt too personal, too close for comfort. But she repeated her question, and I knew I couldn't avoid answering it.

"Yes, I think so," I admitted.

"He's the first, isn't he?" she inquired.

"You're getting cold," I deflected, noticing the raised hairs on her forearm as the wind picked up, causing her to shiver in the dusk.

"Why don't you have a man?" I countered, channelling the defence tactics Mutti had taught me.

Kirstie remained silent, gazing into the valley below.

So, I pressed on, as Mutti had taught me to do. "Why don't you have anybody to love?"

I didn't mean for it to come out spitefully, but it did.

Her response surprised me. I had expected a defensive answer, an excuse, or a joke. Instead, there was a resignation in her tone, an acceptance of the hopelessness she felt.

"It just wasn't meant to be. I have nobody. Nobody but my cats and my horse, and that's why I'm so fucking lonely at times," she confessed, her words tinged with a heart-breaking sigh. I felt an overwhelming urge to embrace her, but I restrained myself.

"There must have been someone. I researched your surname. Bowen-Wright isn't your maiden name, is it?" I probed, trying to uncover more.

"Ahh, the magic of the Internet," she responded dismissively. Then she continued, "There was someone, someone a long time ago. But he let me down. They all let you down in the end."

"What was his name?" I asked, watching her struggle to retrieve the name from her memories.

"Marky. His name was Marky, and he was a complete shit," she revealed.

"I would have punished him if he had left me after only a few years of marriage," I said, pushing ahead.

"Oh, he didn't leave me. I left him. He betrayed me. But how did you know we had only been together a few years?" she questioned.

"Sorry, I just guessed," I lied, knowing that she saw through it. But she didn't press further. After a few moments of silence, she opened up a little more.

"Well, there was one, or maybe there still is one. His name is Gus," she shared.

"Tell me about him," I encouraged her, sensing her sudden animation. But deep down, I already knew everything. Mutti was meticulous in her research.

Suddenly, she became energised and began to tell me about her South African on-off lover. I listened intently, as if hearing it for the first time.

"Why didn't you take him in?" I asked, unable to contain my curiosity.

"Guilt," she replied simply.

"Guilt," she repeated and started picking at her nails.

"Why?" I pressed.

"One day, maybe I'll tell you," she responded, her voice filled with a mix of reluctance and vulnerability.

Then, abruptly changing the subject, she asked, "Wills. Please don't hurt him. He's been through a lot, and he's a lovely lad."

Her words stung me. If it had come from anyone else, it would have sparked anger within me. But her plea revealed just how much she cared for him.

"I promise,"

"Thanks," she acknowledged, and the topic was closed.

"Look, let's go and have some dinner. You look freezing. Wrap my shawl around you. We can enjoy some warm food and wine," I suggested.

"Oh, if you insist," she replied, smiling. "It would be rude not to taste the local wine."

"Absolutely. It would be very rude," I agreed.

As we made our way back to the riverbank, I couldn't help but feel sorry for her, despite all that Mutti had said about her.

**

When she mentioned we were going to eat in a café, I hadn't anticipated what awaited us. Rossi's Café stood at the bustling intersection of tramways and main roads that criss-crossed the city centre. From the outside, it appeared to be just another large townhouse. But appearances can be deceiving.

Despite the early evening hour, the town was still buzzing with a mix of tourists, university students, and residents. As we stepped into the cool interior of the restaurant, we found it virtually empty. It was that lull period between late lunches and early evening sittings. Immaculate in its decor, the two floors of the restaurant boasted a gallery level on the first floor and an open seating area on the ground, where we chose to sit.

Strangely the café seemed to be filled with women. The only

man present was a weathered old gentleman sitting at a table, slurping soup while attempting to read a newspaper. A scrappy dog pestering him from underneath the table added a touch of comedy to the scene. At intervals, he would bribe the dog with pieces of bread. I couldn't help but smile, and he returned the gesture before returning to his soup.

Rebecca babbled something in German to the man, and he laughed, pointing at the dog, and saying something that made her giggle.

"We've come at the right time. Later, it will get very busy. But this is the hour when women come here to meet, talk, and complain about their husbands," she explained.

"Do we wait to be seated?" I inquired.

"No, we can sit anywhere. It's very relaxed," she assured me.

We found a quiet corner, and I made sure to position myself facing the interior so I could people-watch—a habit I've always had, or as Mum would say, being a bit nosey.

Rebecca's words proved true as I surveyed the restaurant. Women in groups held wine glasses, engaged in animated conversations punctuated by tutting, head-shakes, and occasional laughter when something resonated with the group.

"Juice or wine?" Rebecca asked.

"Sorry?"

"Wine or juice? They serve great power juices here," she explained, pointing to the bar where an array of juice cocktails with peculiar names were displayed.

"I think I'll pass. I'll have a small glass of dry white wine," I decided.

She laughed, and soon the waitress arrived to take our orders. I stumbled through my German words, attempting to order my wine, while Rebecca pointed to a fruit cocktail on the board, its name unpronounceable to me. The waitress smiled at my linguistic struggle and responded in English, causing me a twinge of embarrassment.

"They speak many languages here. Most are students at the university," she shared before leaving.

"Why aren't you drinking?" I couldn't help but ask.

"Sorry, I need to keep a clear head. I have things to do later," Rebecca explained.

"Such as?" I pressed, taking my first big gulp from my glass as if my life depended on it.

"Admin, just admin," she replied vaguely.

"For work?" I probed further.

"No, just family stuff," she clarified.

We engaged in light conversation for the next half-hour, fortified by the wine. Then, feeling emboldened, I decided to ask her about her mother.

"Tell me about your mother. She seems nice," I inquired.

Rebecca gave me what seemed like her standard response, explaining that her mother was from the East and worked in administrative tasks for the German government, if one could call it that. But I already knew all of this. Gus had filled me in.

The waitress returned to take our orders. I attempted to order with my limited knowledge of German, resulting in a comical mix of mispronunciations and guesswork.

"Do you even know what you've just ordered?" she asked, chuckling.

I shook my head, laughing along. "I haven't a clue! But I'm sure it will be wonderful."

Rebecca laughed in response, and when the food finally arrived, it surpassed my expectations—rich, warm, and full of gamy flavours. I had guessed correctly. Over the next hour, we chatted about various topics, often revolving around horses. I consciously avoided bringing up Mutti again.

However, it was clear that her thoughts were consumed by Wills. Some of the things I asked her barely registered; she was lost in the realm of infatuation. Was I jealous? Perhaps. But she was my daughter, and I wanted her to be happy.

I had another glass of wine, a generous one at Rebecca's insistence. When I returned from the rest-room, the pudding was waiting for me.

"This is my mother's favourite," Rebecca announced.

"Oh, pudding?" I hesitated.

"You must try the apple strudel. It's the specialty of the house," she insisted.

"Well, I don't usually..." I began to protest, but my objections evaporated as soon as I saw the dessert. Layers of crisp pastry sat on an oversized plate, surrounded by passion fruit and vanilla custard.

"Strudel's lovely," I mumbled, eagerly digging into the hot pastry.

I took another sip of wine and immediately felt light-headed. Perhaps I had indulged too much. There was a peculiar taste in my mouth, and I sensed another social embarrassment looming. But at this point, I was accustomed to such moments and didn't particularly care.

"Sorry, I'm a bit tipsy," I confessed, struggling to articulate the words.

Rebecca smiled and held my hand. "No problem. You've been through a lot lately."

I didn't respond. From the look in her eyes, I could tell she was deep in thought.

The next part is a complete blur. I can't even recall who paid the bill.

As we stepped out of the restaurant, the cool air hit me, and everything started spinning. Trams, cars, and street-lights merged into a kaleidoscope of colours. It felt as if I were on a Ferris wheel, the world spinning round and round. I held onto Rebecca's arm to steady myself on the steps. Everything seemed to be swirling. I saw Rebecca laughing, and all the sights and sounds blended together in a chaotic symphony.

"I'm sorry... Can we get some fresh air?" I managed to mumble, struggling to form the words.

She looked at me, and for a fleeting moment, it seemed like she was sneering.

"Of course. Let's walk by the river, across the Altbrücke. I have something to show you, something I need to do," she replied.

I felt the urge to vomit, but I swallowed hard and held it back. It didn't work.

**

In truth, I'm no different from the rest. I've come to realise that I am just like everyone else, another victim ensnared by my mother's grasp. For far too long, the sword has swung back and forth over my head. But now, I had decided that this would be the last time I would endure her 'encouragement.' Mutti never used the real term for it, never referred to it as what it truly was: blackmail. She always called it 'a little needed encouragement.'

During my teenage years, I began sleeping with her clients, using it as a means of blackmail. Mutti convinced me that it was justifiable since I was supporting the cause, the Communist cause that she believed in so fervently. However, it seamlessly became a form of blackmail against me. I was never a prostitute, never. I was a good girl. But suddenly, I found myself trapped by my own mother, desperate to please her. The only thing stronger than the fire of socialism burning within her heart was her hatred of men and, beyond that, her absolute loathing of Kirstie Bowen-Wright: doctor and murderer.

How did I cope? I developed the ability to hold two completely contradictory and opposing views of the real world simultaneously. They were like separate rooms in my head, and I could choose to inhabit either one, but never both. Now, the barrier between these rooms was beginning to crumble. There was a third version of the world emerging—a third room. In this room, the others could never exist. Occupying this room was becoming more and more appealing with each passing day. It was the world of Will. It was the world of me.

This would be my first and perhaps final refusal for Mutti. I knew how she would label it—refusal of duty for the cause. She would see it as treachery, deceit. But for me, it was liberation, closure, and an end to the lies. I would meet her halfway, or at least in her view, halfway to falling short of her expectations. Kirstie was important to her, but she was more important to me. Kirstie offered a pathway to a better life, a new life, a life with Will—a third room.

When they exchanged glances at the stable, it was the only time I had seen Mutti uncomfortable. No, uncomfortable isn't the right word. Uncertain. She looked uncertain, and I had never witnessed that before. I didn't know what hold she had over Kirstie, but she assured me that it was strong enough to prevent any trouble from arising after the final punishment had been delivered. Mutti was usually right about these things.

Now, I wasn't so sure.

**

I had never felt so embarrassed in my life. I couldn't determine if it was the wine or the exhaustion of it all, but I felt utterly wasted. As we walked across the bridge, I held onto her arm tightly to steady myself. I gripped her so hard that I was in danger of pulling her down with me, tumbling down the steps. At the apex of the crossing, we paused, stood, and watched as a barge passed beneath us. All I could hear was the rumble of the engine and the gentle lapping of the waves as the vessel ploughed through the water, leaving behind swirls and eddies. These sparkled under the night-lights of the bridge before collapsing back into the blackness of the water, disappearing.

We stood there quietly together, and the cool night air brought some relief. I tried to clear my mind, attempting to regain my composure.

"Are you feeling better?" she asked.

"Yes, a bit. I'm sorry. It must have been something I ate earlier,"

I replied.

"I've told you before, don't be sorry. You're my guest," she assured me.

"Thanks," I replied, taking another deep breath of the night air.

I closed my eyes, feeling the breeze brushing against my cheeks. In the distance, I could barely hear the hum of the barge as it blended into the silence of the night. When I opened my eyes, its beacons had disappeared into the darkness, and it was gone. Bizarrely, I felt like a teenager who had stumbled home drunk, embarrassed in front of her parents. Ironically, it was now the other way around.

"Come on, you silly woman. I have something to show you, and then let's get you off to bed," she said.

"Sorry?" I questioned, momentarily confused.

Rebecca didn't respond but took hold of my arm and pulled me across the bridge as if being chased.

"Sorry, can we slow down?" I pleaded.

But she wasn't listening and continued to drag me along the footpath. The path was lined with unfamiliar trees, casting eerie shadows onto the ground. They criss-crossed under my feet, tempting me to fall. Rebecca ran faster and faster until we finally stumbled down a flight of steps in the darkness. Before I could protest any further, we came to a stop. Rebecca held me with both hands and asked gently, "Are you okay?"

I struggled to find my voice, but it failed me.

"I have to do something," she continued, not waiting for my response. She leant me against a shallow stone wall that seemed to materialise out of nowhere, providing support.

The colours around me merged, and the sounds blended into one. The past became the present. I felt an uncontrollable urge to vomit once again.

Then, she thrust it in front of me.

I flinched.

"It's a lock! Our lock!" she exclaimed.

"What...?" I managed to utter.

"A love-lock!" she replied, excitement in her voice.

She pushed it closer to me, and I tilted my head back, squinting to merge the two blurry images into one. It was a padlock. I squinted harder, trying to make out the words etched on the front: *Wills* ♥ *Rebecca*. She stared at me, grinning like an infatuated child.

"This one has a little chamber where you can put a key or a special message. I've put one in!" she explained eagerly.

She then spun around and attached it to what appeared to be a sandstone pillar covered in brass rings, each encasing a thousand similar locks of various sizes, colours, and shapes. They were all different, yet even in my stupor, I could see that they all bore the same message—a declaration of the nonsensical, irrational, crazy love between two people.

Feeling myself slipping away, I pressed my back firmly against the wall, feeling its stony edges. I strangely felt nothing but a gentle warmth at the base of my spine. I pressed harder, doing everything I could to remain upright, to avoid collapsing and letting my daughter down. I could feel myself swaying from side to side as her words washed over me like the waves on the shore—clear one moment, then gone the next. Her voice blended with the other noises around me—the lapping of the water against the riverbank, the laughter of people in the night. I tried to focus on Rebecca. She looked so beautiful, so radiant in the light, like an angel.

She handed me the key.

"You keep it safe," she urged.

I clasped it tightly in my palm, holding onto it with all my strength.

"It's a special message. One day, you'll open it. Promise?" she asked.

I promised.

"I trust you. Keep it," she concluded.

That was the last thing I remember from that night.

**

The darkness gradually gave way to a dull grey, which then dissipated into a dim fog, engulfing the poorly lit and shuttered room. I awoke, feeling confused. Bizarre and nonsensical dreams faded into a sense of uncertainty about my surroundings. I was unsure if I was asleep and dreaming of being awake, or barely awake and caught in the hazy realm between consciousness and slumber. Gradually, the mist began to lift.

My hands and feet, previously weighed down by an underwater force in a dream, now felt heavy and restrained, bound to a chair with makeshift bindings. As my senses sharpened, I became aware of the dryness in my mouth—an unpleasant taste of cheap alcohol, spoiled food, and vomit. I strained to hear any sounds, but there was nothing but silence, broken only by the rhythm of my own heartbeat and breathing.

Surveying the room, I found it devoid of furniture, as empty as a deserted shell. The bare floorboards lay exposed, while torn and peeling wallpaper hung from the walls. The pervasive smell of dampness mingled with that of neglected garden sheds.

Then, with the distinct sound of stiletto heels striking the wooden floor, she entered. The scene before me became clear—a portrait of my daughter standing expressionless in front of me. In her right hand, swinging gently back and forth, she held a blade.

A smile crossed her face.

Finally, as if she had rehearsed the words a thousand times, she began to tell the story.

Chapter 16

When she finished speaking, I felt utterly broken, and confused. The room seemed to close in on me, and I struggled to breathe. I was certain the walls were moving. None of her words made any sense. I felt bewildered, trapped. The warmth and dampness at the base of my back indicated sweat and an unpleasant smell of stale urine emanated from my lap. The noise around me merged into a single hum, blending my mother's scolding, my father's loving words, and my baby's gentle coos. Then the voices faded away, and the walls felt like they were closing in, pressing closer and closer. It had to be a dream, I desperately believed if I could just push through, I would be free.

But it wasn't a dream and my stomach became filled with a hollow, sickening panic. Uncontrollably, I began to scream, my voice reaching an ear-piercing pitch. It felt as if someone else was screaming, not me. I squeezed my eyes shut tightly and continued to cry out, as if by some miracle it would make everything vanish.

But it didn't.

Her palm struck me with such force that I toppled sideways, crashing to the floor, my temple colliding with the unforgiving floorboards. Suddenly, the world tilted, and all I could see were the glistening knife and my daughter's stiletto heels.

Rushing over, she lifted me upright, and the clatter of the knife echoed as it came to a standstill on the floor.

"I'm sorry," she cried, appearing shocked what she had done.

"I'm sorry, she made me do it." she repeated.

Just as I was about to break into another cry, she pressed a finger against my lips.

"It's no use. Nobody can hear us. We're far away from anyone," she whispered.

I looked up at her. She looked distraught. I felt something warm trickling down my cheek, staining my dress crimson.

"It can't be true. I don't know anything. I don't remember anything happening," I stammered, tears stinging my eyes.

"Mutti said it was so," she whispered back.

Sniffling, I continued to shed tears, unable to grasp the reality of it all.

"Why do you hate me?" I uttered slowly, emphasizing each word.

I stared at my daughter, who turned away nervously, playing with her hair.

"I don't hate you," she responded.

"My mother hates you," she added, avoiding eye contact.

"She wants to see you."

"Do you always do everything your mother says?" I questioned, noticing doubt flickering in her eyes.

She tugged her hair behind her ear and looked away once more.

"No," she admitted in a hushed voice. "Not anymore."

"I'm hurting and angry," she added defensively, her agitation growing. She paced back and forth, her hand pressed against her mouth in worry, resembling a child who had realised the gravity of their actions. She repeatedly dragged her hair over her scalp.

"Untie me. We can talk ?"

She looked down at my bindings. I could see doubt in her eyes.

"No. Mutti said not to."

"What was that for ?" I asked, signalling to the blade.

"Muti said to hurt you."

Then it dawned on me.

"Make you just like me. Then you'd know what it felt like," she said.

She turned away again.

"Why? Why would she want to do that ?"

"Look, all I want to do is do what Mutti wants. Do what Mutti wants and move on," she replied.

She became more and more agitated, and paced short steps, back and forth, and held her hand against her mouth with worry, like a child who had realised they had done something very bad. She dragged her hair over her scalp, again and again.

I pressed on.

"Do you love your mother?" I asked, awaiting her response.

There was a pause, and then she met my gaze.

"Of course, why wouldn't I?" she answered.

"If you had a daughter, if you and Wills ever had a daughter, would you love her? Would you ever hurt her?" I questioned further.

"Of course not," she practically grinned.

"Then how could your 'dearest, darling Mutti' hurt her own daughter?" I asked.

"What?" she murmured; confusion evident in her voice.

"How could any mother take a blade to her only child, disfigure her, mutilate her?" I challenged, watching as her gaze fell to her finger.

"I'm sorry?" she managed to interject, but I was already too far gone. Consumed by decades of built-up anger, words erupted from me in a torrent, a visceral release. They poured out, fuelled by my gut-wrenching fury, as if the act of speaking them would bring some semblance of closure, regardless of the consequences.

"You're my FUCKING DAUGHTER! I don't give a shit about your Mutti. That woman is an evil, spiteful BITCH!" I screamed, drowning out her attempted interjection. My fury escalated, and I continued to yank at the restraints, consumed by rage.

"Your mother has tormented me for over thirty years. She has hounded me, persecuted me, made me break every oath I made as a doctor. Everything that was important to me, everything that defined who I was. She turned my own child against me, disfigured her, and I still don't know what the FUCK I've done wrong!"

The words flowed relentlessly, like a volcanic eruption, and I gasped for breath, my chest heaving. Then, as suddenly as the outpouring began, the room was filled with a deafening silence. My breath calmed to a gentle gasp.

My daughter stared at me unbelieving it fully. She shook her head.

Abruptly, she retreated with cautious steps, her head bowed. Without even looking at me, she left the room.

205

"Find the answers in my room!" I shouted after her, before she was gone.

Silence enveloped me once more. The only sounds were now my own breathing and the pounding in my head. I noticed a steaming pool of water rolling across the floor, but I no longer cared. I sat and waited for her return,

**

I knew I couldn't go through with it, yet I didn't even attempt to. Mutti would be furious, but I couldn't bring myself to do it. All I desired in that moment was to escape, even though it meant I wouldn't see Wills again. What she had revealed left me shocked and utterly confused. Wills had sent me a text, asking how I was, but I couldn't muster a reply. I trembled with terror, my entire being shook.

Leaving the farmhouse, I leant against the car. The sky weighed heavy with storm clouds, swollen from the day's warmth. Rain began to fall, accompanied by the distant crack of thunder. The sky darkened, silencing the birdsong.

For nearly an hour, I remained outside seeking shelter beneath a leaking canopy as the sky grew increasingly ominous. I stood there, gazing at everything and nothing. I didn't know what to do.

Signs of a half-hearted attempt at renovation surrounded me— overturned, rusting cement mixers forgotten amidst piles of discarded building materials. The rain turned the ground filthy. Vague memories resurfaced of the old woman who once lived here, a distant figure from my childhood holidays. We used to call her 'Die Hexe,' or The Witch. I recalled how she frightened us with her scowls as we crossed her farmland as a short-cut to school. One day, she even spat at us, ensuring we never ventured that way again. Even now, the place filled me with discomfort.

Lost in thought, I stood there, contemplating everything, accompanied by the rhythmic patter of rain. None of it made sense. I had to go and see for myself and understand if it were true.

**

The air grew heavy, and the room darkened. I could faintly hear the distant rumble of thunder, followed by the tapping of raindrops on the skylight, gradually intensifying into a percussive rhythm. Closing my eyes, I focused on the sound, hoping the water's drumming against the glass would distract me.

The ache in my back resurfaced. Thoughts of escaping my bindings briefly crossed my mind. However, in the cold reality of the moment, I simply couldn't muster the effort. Exhausted, I listened to the hypnotic sound of the rain and drifted off to sleep. It felt like mere moments, yet the sleep seemed longer. I was awakened by the sound of a door latch, followed by a squeak as it closed. Slow, deliberate footsteps followed, almost shuffling in nature.

"Rebecca?" I whispered, expecting to see my daughter. But it wasn't.

It was her.

"Why did you return? We had an understanding," she spoke, her voice lacking any softness. Her words were precise and direct.

I didn't respond, but instead stared at her, taken aback by how small she appeared after all these years.

"We had an understanding," she repeated, standing before me.

I silently chuckled at how aged she looked, weathered by the absence of love, deprived of the experience of holding someone close and truly loving them.

For a few seconds, we locked eyes, glowering at each other.

"Maybe you need a little more encouragement. My daughter is important to me. I want to ensure she isn't harmed," she continued, her words deliberate and slow, as if addressing a child.

I couldn't bear it any longer.

"You are a complete and utter evil... BITCH!" I screamed, but she didn't even flinch. She simply offered a mocking smile.

She shuffled closer to me, picking up the blade from the floor. Her nose crinkled in distaste as she looked at the pool of urine.

"Where is she?"

207

I remained silent.

"Where is my daughter?" she persisted, casually waving the knife before me.

I erupted again.

"She's, my daughter. My FUCKING daughter! MY child!"

My body shook as if in a spasm, yet she didn't even blink.

She stepped closer and continued.

"We had a promise. You broke your promise. It seems to be a recurring weakness of yours—a self-indulgent weakness. I truly believed you were made of sterner stuff, Kirstie," and as she uttered my name, I winced at the familiarity.

A sense of emptiness washed over me as she loomed above me. The silence became almost unbearable. Gathering my thoughts, I struggled to find my voice. After what felt like an eternity of nothingness, I closed my eyes and asked her the question.

"Why have you tormented me all these years? Why did you take her? I just need to know," I pleaded, my spirit shattered by the futility of it all, worn down by a lifetime of emotional attrition at the hands of a woman standing just a few feet away. I had thought about this wretched woman every single day since she took my daughter, every day since her crib grew cold.

And now she was here.

"You don't remember, do you? Surely, you remember?" she whispered. I opened my eyes and could see she was crying. She glanced down at the knife, then back up at me.

"Rebecca, I will finish the job. You bad girl." she muttered to herself.

Slowly, she ran the blade over my knuckle.

It was an unassuming manilla folder that I had torn the room apart searching for. Eventually, I discovered it concealed in a false lining of her suitcase, deliberately hidden to be found. My hands trembled as I sat on her bed, taking a deep breath. I thought I knew what lay inside, but I was gravely mistaken. With shaky hands, I emptied its contents onto the bed, and a cascade of photographs spilled out.

They were all pictures of me: moments on the boat with Mutti, my first and last day at school, snapshots from my graduation from Medical School. Laughter frozen in time before my father's departure. In each one, I appeared so happy. I had been happy then. On the back of each photograph, there was a date and a little message inscribed in Mutti's distinctive spidery handwriting.

Then I saw the letter, adorned with crimson stains and bearing my mother's name at the bottom. I stared at it, unsure what it was. Behind it was something else.

It was a the lab report. I studied it.

It outlined a comparison of specimens, a report familiar to me from my university days: mitochondrial DNA profiling conducted to establish genetic links between individuals.

I read the conclusion: *The probability of individual A & B being identical by chance = 1 x 10^{-9} (Classification: Improbable). The probability of B & C maternal linkage being by chance = 0.5 x 10^{-9} (Classification: Improbable).*

Rushing to the end, I searched for the key.

Sample ID:	Specimen	Name
62727738: A	Blood on paper	Unknown
63738398: B	Hair	Rebecca Mueller
77738890: C	Serum sample	Kirstie Bowen-Wright

Sitting on the bed, I tried to comprehend it all.

I re-read the faded letter, which spoke of '*a present to give me encouragement.*' Deep down, it held the truth.

Gazing outside, I noticed that the storm had finally subsided, making way for a bright and refreshing sky. I made my way to the kitchen, and found what I needed.

**

"Wait! Wait! I need to know," I screeched, the words bursting from my lips.

She paused, driving the blade into the floorboard with a dull thud, and took a step back. Leaning in so close that I could feel her breath on my face, she began to speak.

With deliberate and measured words, she unveiled the truth.

"Rebecca was not my only daughter," she revealed. "No. There was another, my first child. The one you took away. The one you sent to a place from which nobody returns."

Overwhelmed, I closed my eyes, unable to meet her gaze any longer.

"We tried for years to conceive," she continued.

"But eventually, the doctors in East Germany diagnosed me. They said there was no hope. I was devastated, shattered. He didn't understand."

"Do you know what it's like to be unable to have a child? Do you?" she asked coldly.

I opened my eyes and glared at her.

She smiled back at me, taking a shallow breath before resuming her narrative.

"Then the Wall came down. It was 1989, and it was horrible," she declared vehemently.

"But Germany was reunified," I murmured.

"Nein! It was disgusting," she erupted, her voice filled with bitterness. "I had to fight. They needed to be punished. We were being betrayed. They were stupid, all stupid."

She stared into the distance, her gaze piercing through me, before collecting her thoughts and pacing back and forth.

"But amidst all that, one good thing happened. We moved to England. I had some business to attend to, some unfinished matters. We spent every penny, all the money we had saved. It was a new treatment. And eventually, she was born. One of the first. Technology liberated me from my sterility."

"Her name was Suzanna. She had fair hair and a beautiful smile. I loved her so much. She was the one who mattered," she revealed, her voice filled with a mixture of love and pain.

Curiosity overwhelmed me, and I asked, "What happened?"

"You killed her," she replied coldly.

Her words hit me like a hard slap.

She took a deep sigh of a breath and continued.

"She was still a babe in arms. One night, before we were due to return, she became feverish, ill, sweating. My husband said it was nothing, a chill. But I refused to listen. We had gone so far to have her. We took her to the hospital. I demanded to be seen."

She began to weep.

"I screamed for hours to be seen. Eventually they let her be treated. She…"

She was struggling to get the words out. She knelt beside me and laid her head on my lap, and muttered to herself in German before continuing.

"Then a busy doctor, said it would be all right. It was nothing, nothing but a cold."

I could feel my eyes filling up.

After an age during which I could hear nothing but my breathlessness and her mumbling in German, she went on.

" She died two days later. It was meningitis. A further two days later she was burnt away and was gone. "

"I'm really, really sorry. But I don't remember, " I murmured.

She sat up and looked at me. Her tear-stained eyes glinted in the dim light. I had to look away.

"I'm sorry... I don't remember." I whispered.

211

"Why did you take my baby from me?" I asked softly.

She stood up, leaning closer to whisper in my ear, "Because I could."

A tear trickled down my cheek as her words sank in.

"...and torment me with the games?" I questioned, my voice trembling.

" Because of what you did. I had to take away your promise. I had to strip away your oath, line by line," she declared, her words piercing through me.

Shaking in my seat, straining against my bindings, I desperately pulled at the cords. Tears cascaded down my cheeks.

She took a step back.

"Don't cry. Your daughter is nothing. You can have her. She is nothing but dirty, damaged goods. She will never replace Suzanna, ever."

"But she is still, MINE ! " I erupted

" ..and always will be. You FUCKING BITCH ! "

She coldly looked at me. I remember she didn't even flinch.

"Yes, you can have her. " she said matter-of-factly.

"She has turned herself into nothing but a common whore. See how shallow she has become, wallowing in her gutter of immorality ? "

"But she is *mine*." I repeated.

"Have her back. My job is done. You are broken, and your daughter is broken, broken and soiled. She will never be clean again."

Both of us looked at each other in silence and hatred.

Then suddenly cutting through everything, she returned.

With the clip-clop of stilettos on wood, and my daughter entered the room with the grace and composure of a model on the catwalk.

At that moment, everything paused as we both stared at each other. In life a circle is sometimes completed, a circle you never knew existed. The end becomes the beginning, and the beginning becomes the end.

Mutti stood up.

"Meine Tochter, where have you been ? Your friend and myself were just in discussion."

Rebecca held up her middle finger to her.

And for once Mutti said nothing. Rebecca stopped and rocked on her heels, her face emotionless and empty.

"Why Mutti? Why did you do it? "

"Because," she repeated with less bravado.

"Because? It's as simple as that?" Rebecca asked coldly.

The woman looked flustered, wiped her face and turned away from her.

"I needed to hate, to keep going. I had to do it. To make you in my image."

"And that's why you blackmailed even me...your only daughter ?"

Mutti said nothing.

"No, that's incorrect," Rebecca added after a pause.

"You blackmailed somebody else's daughter, blackmailed them into becoming - a common prostitute."

"It was for the cause, " Mutti muttered.

Rebecca erupted.

"Do you know how many men - stinking, filthy men - I have FUCKED to support your cause ? Nein ? Fucked and degraded in every possible way. At times I felt my very soul being pushed out of me with every grunt those bastards made."

Mutti glared at the insolence of her question.

Rebecca exhaled a breath, almost spent of her dying anger.

"It is over. I want no more of it. Let her go. You have destroyed so much. I want to be happy now. I want to be me."

"...with that stupid farmer-boy of yours ? How sweet."

Then before she could say anymore, the circle became complete.

Looking back I'd play the next few seconds over and over in my mind for the rest of my life. They say that at crucial moments, time slows to a standstill and new futures are made.

213

Rebecca reached within her blouse and pulled out a blade. A millisecond later Mutti tugged the knife free from the floor. Everything moved frame by

single frame.

"Verdammte Schlampe!"

Mutti screamed and lunged forward.

My daughter swung down the blade.

Then it was over.

At that time, I thought it was a crack of thunder. Then I saw a tingle of glass flashing to a red centre on Mutti's forehead. Then an envelope of bone, blood and brain escaping from the back of her skull with the sound of a sigh.

Rebecca dropped the knife.

Mutti collapsed to the floor with a thud.

I remember descending into a scream, a scream so strong I finally broke my bindings.

My daughter stood and stared, and said nothing, nothing but the mouthing of words in German, caught in her own world.

The next was a blur, a jumble of voices shouting, the trample of boots, policemen, medics yelling and bizarrely, Gus.

He stood in front of me. I vaguely remember him attempting to kiss me and in that moment, I didn't know whether it was just another chapter of a bad dream unfolding.

Chapter 17

Epilogue - Two months later

Nervously, I picked at my nails, a habit I had fallen back into. It was a disgusting habit, and I knew it. Ordering another tonic water, I waited anxiously. The barman flashed me a smile, probably thinking I was a woman on her first date in years. Mutton dressed up as mutton, as Mum would have said. I smiled back, hoping not to appear too desperate.

I had done my best to prepare for this meeting. I had splurged on an expensive haircut, spending nearly two hours in the salon. Two bloody hours for a haircut? But it did look good, the mess of red curls from a bottle at least made me presentable. For the first time in years, I felt feminine.

The wine-bar was nearly empty, and I could feel the barman's eyes on me. Where was he? Would he come? He promised he would and that he would explain everything.

I hadn't seen Gus since Heidelberg when he disappeared as quickly as he had appeared. He had apologised as I was being taken to the ambulance, slipping his card into my hand. The card bore a message on the back, finished with kisses.

Just when I was about to give up hope, he finally arrived.

"Sorry, I'm running a bit late. Bloody students always want a piece of me after lectures," Gus apologised.

"Gus, I was getting worried. I was starting to think you wouldn't come," I admitted, relief washing over me.

"...and just stand you up? Usually, it's the other way around," he said with a wink.

"No," was all I managed to say.

Gus fetched himself a drink from the bar. I looked at him as he leant against the counter, engaging in a conversation with the barman about the rugby match on the television screen. From behind, he looked strong, his hair slightly thinning on the top but otherwise intact. I made a mental note to tease him about it later.

He sat down across from me. "Not drinking?" he asked.

I swirled the tonic water in my glass, attempting to make it look more interesting. "No, I decided it wasn't doing me any good anymore."

He remained silent for a moment before sighing heavily. "How's Rebecca? Is she okay?"

"Yes, she's fine. She didn't say anything for the first few days. Finding out your boss is suddenly your bloody mother could really mess you up. But she's strong, she'll get through it."

"Strong, just like her mother," he commented, causing me to look away, feeling slightly embarrassed.

"We're taking it slowly, day-by-day, small steps. Wills has been great. Those two are so utterly in love, and I'm sure it helps," I replied.

He didn't say anything.

We spent the next half-hour engaging in small talk and exchanging pleasantries, tiptoeing around the big issue at hand. Gradually, I began to relax.

Finally, we delved into the purpose of our meeting, amongst other things.

"She asked me how the police sniper missed her. I'm sure she feels guilty about it all," I confided.

"He wasn't aiming for her," Gus stated flatly. "They got who they wanted, in one clean shot. They were just waiting for an opportunity."

"Who?"

"The German Secret Service,"

His words hit me like a cold wave. I gave him a hard stare and unleashed my frustration.

"Look, for fuck's sake, Gus! Put all your cards on the bloody table for once."

He placed his beer glass down with a thud. "And will you? Or are you going to spin me another tale of crap and brush me away like before?"

"Okay, okay," I conceded, continuing to dig at my nails.

"Is this why you've been avoiding me all these years?" he continued, frustration pouring out.

"Yes," I replied, speaking the truth for the first time in nearly thirty years. "I couldn't tell anyone. I was too scared. It would have hurt her. I needed to carry it all myself. I was her mother. I made an oath to protect her, and I failed. It was all my fault."

"Look, Kirstie, life is just a series of chance episodes. Look at me," Gus said, taking a sip of his drink.

I took a sip of mine as well. "Do you know what, Gus? I'm so happy she's dead. How horrible is that? That's what I've become."

"By all accounts, she was a nasty piece of work," he remarked, and I couldn't deny that.

"What I don't understand is how she always knew where I was. Wherever I went, she always found me,"

"I told her," he replied without hesitation.

His words hit me. I didn't know whether to slap him or walk out. I did neither. I needed to know, to tie up the loose ends of the disaster and move on.

He sighed and took another swig of his beer. "Before I became a nurse of sorts, I was an Intelligence Officer in South Africa. After I left, they approached me."

"Who?" I inquired.

"Stasi, the East German Intelligence Service. And after the Wall fell, it was the German Republic who came calling."

"Shit. You're a bloody spy?" I exclaimed.

"Was a bloody spy. I've only recently told them all to fuck off and leave me alone,"

"How long has this been going on?"

"Thirty years, just after Mueller went rogue," he revealed, leaving me in stunned silence, unable to comprehend it all.

"Sorry. I did it to protect you,"

"SORRY? Protect me? By allowing that monstrous woman to fuck up my entire life?" I exclaimed.

Other customers began to stare. Gus signalled to the barman

to let him know we were just having a little domestic. He leaned closer, continuing in his hushed but forceful tone.

"Ingrid Mueller was extremely dangerous, a lone spy with a burning hatred of the reunification. You weren't the only one. She pushed scores of individuals to their deaths. It reached the highest levels of the government. Even the Chancellor was under suspicion. Their Secret Service had been tracking her for years. But she was always one step ahead. One crafty, devious bitch."

"You don't need to tell me that," I muttered.

"Sorry,"

"Look, it worked both ways. I was a South African contact with Stasi. I was able to track her," he explained.

I didn't know what to say.

"You were never in danger. German Intelligence was always there. How do you think we got out of Rwanda so easily that night? How did Rebecca miraculously apply for the position you advertised to the agency? Why would a German medic in Southern Germany be interested in a practice position in a small, sleepy coastal town in England unless she was offered a very lucrative sweetener? We just needed Rebecca to flush her mother out."

I thought it through and continued to dig at my nails. "I'm her mother," I replied tartly.

"Sorry"

"They helped, but they couldn't interfere. They needed proof. You gave them the proof to finally take action," Gus clarified.

He didn't have to explain what 'take action' really meant.

"So what's going to happen now?" I asked, feeling overwhelmed.

"The German government has drawn a line under the matter. It's as if it never happened,"

"Shit. Jesus Fucking Christ!"

"I'm sorry, but you will have to leave, if you can't keep it down," the barman shouted at us.

Now it was my turn to placate him with a mouthed, sorry.

We both sat there in silence, each nursing our own personal

hurt. Mine was the realisation that my life had been completely messed up, and I had participated in a pantomime I was completely unaware of.

I could see the glistening in Gus's eyes. "I fucking loved you, K. Loved you so much. Since that night in Cape Town, you've been tearing me apart, pushing me away."

Suddenly, he leant over and kissed me. It was the last thing I expected.

"I've been waiting to do that for years."

He collapsed back into his seat, his face beginning to crumple. I wiped my eyes and began to sob.

"I'm really, really sorry," I managed to say, my words interspersed with tears. He reached over and clasped my hand, and it felt so good. In the corner of my eye, I could see the blurred figure of the barman staring at us. But I didn't care. I didn't give a fuck.

"Do you like cats?" I asked, my words slipping out between sobs.

"What?" Gus questioned.

"I said, do you like cats?"

"I love cats," he replied.

I leant over and kissed him.

"Of course, I love cats."

"It's bloody horses I can't stand,"

I wanted to slap him. But I was crying too much.

Eventually, we were asked to leave the bar.

So we did.

Hand in hand.

Six months later

As the clouds parted, the sun emerged at the perfect moment, casting a radiant glow on the statue of Hercules in the Market Square. The gilded metal shone brilliantly in the morning summer sun. It was an idyllic scene. The square bustled with a mix of tourists leisurely passing the morning away and wedding guests eagerly awaiting the couple.

All eyes turned to the newly-weds as they exited the Town Hall, pausing for a moment. A ripple of applause spread through the crowd, accompanied by whistles, clapping, and supportive cheers. Amidst the throng, I stood, trying to remain hidden and inconspicuous.

She looked breath-taking in her peach dress. Wills appeared impeccably smart, unable to contain his beaming smile. They giggled and beamed, savouring the moment that would soon become a cherished memory.

Rebecca waved at me, but I pretended not to notice. This was their moment, not mine. Gus put his arm around me, brushing a strand of hair away from my face. She looked so beautiful. I noticed Wills' rugby friends ogling her when he wasn't looking.

"She's a bloody stunner, isn't she? A bloody stunner," Gus exclaimed.

"She's my daughter. Why wouldn't she be? It's in the genes," I playfully replied.

"Absolutely," he agreed sensibly.

Descending the steps, a group of her university friends—I presumed — surrounded her, enveloping her in their excitement. She grabbed two of them by the hand and scurried toward me, Wills trailing obediently behind. She stopped at my feet, bubbling with enthusiasm.

"This is Kirstie, a very close friend of mine from England," she introduced. "And this is Gus. He's her boyfriend."

I think I blushed. Calling Gus my boyfriend made me just feel like a silly girl.

"No, I'm Kirstie's chauffeur, kitchen cook, and general bottle-washer," Gus chimed in.

They all laughed.

"Congratulations. I'm so happy for you. Let me see your ring," I asked, extending my hand.

She offered her hand, adorned with a clean gold band that looked perfect. "Cost me a bloody fortune," Wills remarked, earn-ing a glare from me.

"Not as priceless as the hand wearing it. You take good care of her," I scolded him playfully, almost slipping into calling her my daughter.

"You know I will," he replied before continuing, "The reception is on a cruise boat this afternoon. Though, everyone must wear buoyancy aids, even the bride. Health and safety and all that."

Rebecca shot him a scowl, silently conveying her annoyance.

"Only joking," he sheepishly added.

Rebecca hugged me tightly, leant forward and whispered in my ear so nobody else could hear.

"Thank you, Mum."

Her words brought tears to my eyes. I turned away to discreetly blow my nose, and then they were gone swallowed up by their throng of friends and well-wishers.

That afternoon we spent cruising the Neckar to Hirschon-Neckar, a charming town nestled almost entirely on a river island formed by a hairpin bend. People on the riverbanks waved and shouted as we passed, reminiscent of the way people in England used to do when trains went by.

As the afternoon progressed, Wills' rugby friends grew rowdier and tipsier, fuelled by German beer, dancing clumsily to the traditional 'oompah-pah' music that my daughter had arranged. Yet, despite their boisterousness, every man was simply thrilled to be celebrating the day, revelling in the local hospitality, and engaging in playful banter with the young waitresses; an endearing trait of Welsh boys.

As the afternoon wore on we both found a quiet spot at the stern of the boat, a refuge for the 'old and infirm' as Gus humorously put it. From there, we watched in awe as my daughter danced with Wills on a swaying dance floor. Whenever she seemed on the verge of stumbling, he would swoop in, catching her just in time, and they would both erupt in laughter while her friends clapped to the rhythm of the music.

And then he asked.

In that moment, a lump formed in my throat. The words simply wouldn't come out.

"I said, will you marry me?" he repeated.

Still, the words eluded me.

"Please don't turn me away again. But if you must, then do it."

And then they flowed.

"Of course, I'll bloody marry you! You stupid bugger!" I exclaimed.

I had never seen a man so elated, and I was sure he had never seen a middle-aged woman look the same. I showered him with kisses, with a ferocity that even my daughter noticed.

We spent the next few hours dancing with Rebecca and Wills. I was ecstatic, basking in the glow of pure happiness. As the sun began to sink behind the hill, casting a crescent of light that dwindled into darkness, the band played a slow, gentle tune, breaking the silence.

Later, when I was alone, Rebecca approached me, her face aglow from dancing and the day's festivities. I could hardly contain myself.

"Your mother's getting married!" I exclaimed.

At first, she said nothing, but then realisation dawned.

"Wow!" she screamed.

I burst into giggles. "Yes, he just asked me. I'm bloody over fifty, and I'm getting married!"

"Wunderbar!" she cried, planting a kiss on my cheek. "I'm going to get you a love lock like ours. Like the one I got for Wills, with the message inside for you."

She took a step back, holding me in her arms.

"Sorry?" I asked.

"Remember the lock near the bridge?"

"Yes" I replied, still puzzled.

"No. The message wasn't for him,"

"I just presumed, "

"You have the key. Open it," she said.

And the next morning, I did.

**

I slipped out of the hotel just before dawn, leaving Gus sound asleep, exhausted from a day filled with laughter, copious litres of German beer, and our passionate lovemaking after we returned to our room - all of which he assured me he could handle.

I made my way to the riverbank. Heidelberg was awakening, its sounds and aromas permeating the air—the tantalizing scent of freshly baked goods mingling with the bustling noise of morning coffee shops arranging their street tables. Walking over the cobblestones and across the AltBruke, I savoured the stillness. A cool breeze drifted down the valley, and in the dim light, I glimpsed the sun on the horizon, gradually painting the day with vibrant colours.

Eventually, I stumbled upon the garden she had taken me to, though it appeared blurry in my recollection of that dreadful night.

I meticulously checked countless locks securely fastened to the stonework until I found hers. It was surrounded by a sea of other love messages, and I hesitated, uncertain if it was the right one. But then I read the engraving on its side—a heartfelt message of love.

Placing the key into the chamber, I turned it.

It opened.

I retrieved the message and read it.

Dearest Mother,

These words are nothing more than a worth-
less apology to you if anything should go awry and
the final path is closed. How it will unfold, I do not
know. I only possess fragments, fragments that I am
still endeavouring to piece together as best I can.

No matter what happens, I promise to be the daughter
you never had. I pledge to be a good daughter to you. If
anything goes amiss,

I am truly sorry. Truly sorry for all that has passed.

Your daughter, with eternal love,

Rebecca.

I rolled the message back up, returned it to its place, closed the lock....and smiled.

Standing in the soft glow of the approaching dawn, as the sun heralded another day and fulfilled its promise, I grasped the truth. I realised that as one light is extinguished, another ember of love is often fanned into radiant brilliance.

And so, it was.

Milton Keynes UK
Ingram Content Group UK Ltd.
UKHW050738120224
437693UK00008B/130